The Dragon Mother

and the Azure Dragon Rising

Amy
History 111
Dr. Goldberg
November 22, 1978

Pledge - Amy

High praise for *The Dragon Mother and the Azure Dragon Rising*

"The Dragon Mother and the Azure Dragon Rising is a work of highly enjoyable mythological fiction penned by author David Hansford. This novella-length work is suitable for all ages due to its mild content, as well as stunning illustrations included by the author himself. In this engaging tale, part myth, part spiritual thinking, the origins of dragons and the powerful Dragon Mother are discussed, as well as many tales of encounters with dragons, in disguise or as themselves. The work asks you to be transported to the creative world, setting aside conventional ideas and believing in the reality of dragons along with the author.

It certainly isn't difficult to feel whisked away to a world where dragons are real when you see the enchanting illustrations of author David Hansford. From the first page, those descriptions and depictions are sure to grip readers who appreciate the beauty and mystery of the dragon myth, as well as the photographs of real spiritual practices which can accompany the tales of dragons and their mystic power. David Hansford combines the stories from Chinese dragon mythology with an account of his own meditations and spiritual practices, explaining how a belief in the ancient wisdom of dragons can benefit your lifestyle in many ways. Though the tales are almost like fairy stories in their pleasant narration, the connection with real-world spiritual practices is where this work's real magic lies. Overall, *The Dragon Mother and the Azure Dragon Rising* is a compelling work for the spiritually curious."

— K.C. Finn, award-winning author of more than 25 novels including *The Book of Shade, The Mind's Eye,* and *Legion Lost*

The Dragon Mother
and the Azure Dragon Rising

Printed in U.S.A.
Library of Congress Cataloging
    Hansford, David.
       The Dragon Mother / David Hansford 1st ed.
       ISBN: 978-0-9963458-8-0

Artwork / paintings: David Hansford / davidhansford.com
Art direction: David Hansford / Bending Pine Tree Studio
Book design: Katie Gould / The HillHelen Group LLC
Editor: Jacque Hillman / The HillHelen Group LLC
Photograph of author: Laura Acero-Hansford

Acknowledgments:
    Editing, advice, and layout design by Jacque Hillman and Katie Gould were invaluable, as well as the ideas and encouragement from Laura Acero-Hansford and Cami Nuñez.
    The support through the years from Suzanne Evans, Patricia Parker, and Dr. Sandra Hansford kept the creativity flowing.
    This book and all the artwork would not have happened without the love and assistance of Ann and Amy Bull.
    Deep gratitude to the early 20th century scholars and writers, who focused their abilities on the mythology and culture of Asia — especially Laurence Binyon, Dr. M.W. de Visser, and Ernest Ingersoll.

The HillHelen Group LLC
127 Fairmont Ave., Jackson, TN 38301
hillhelengroup@gmail.com

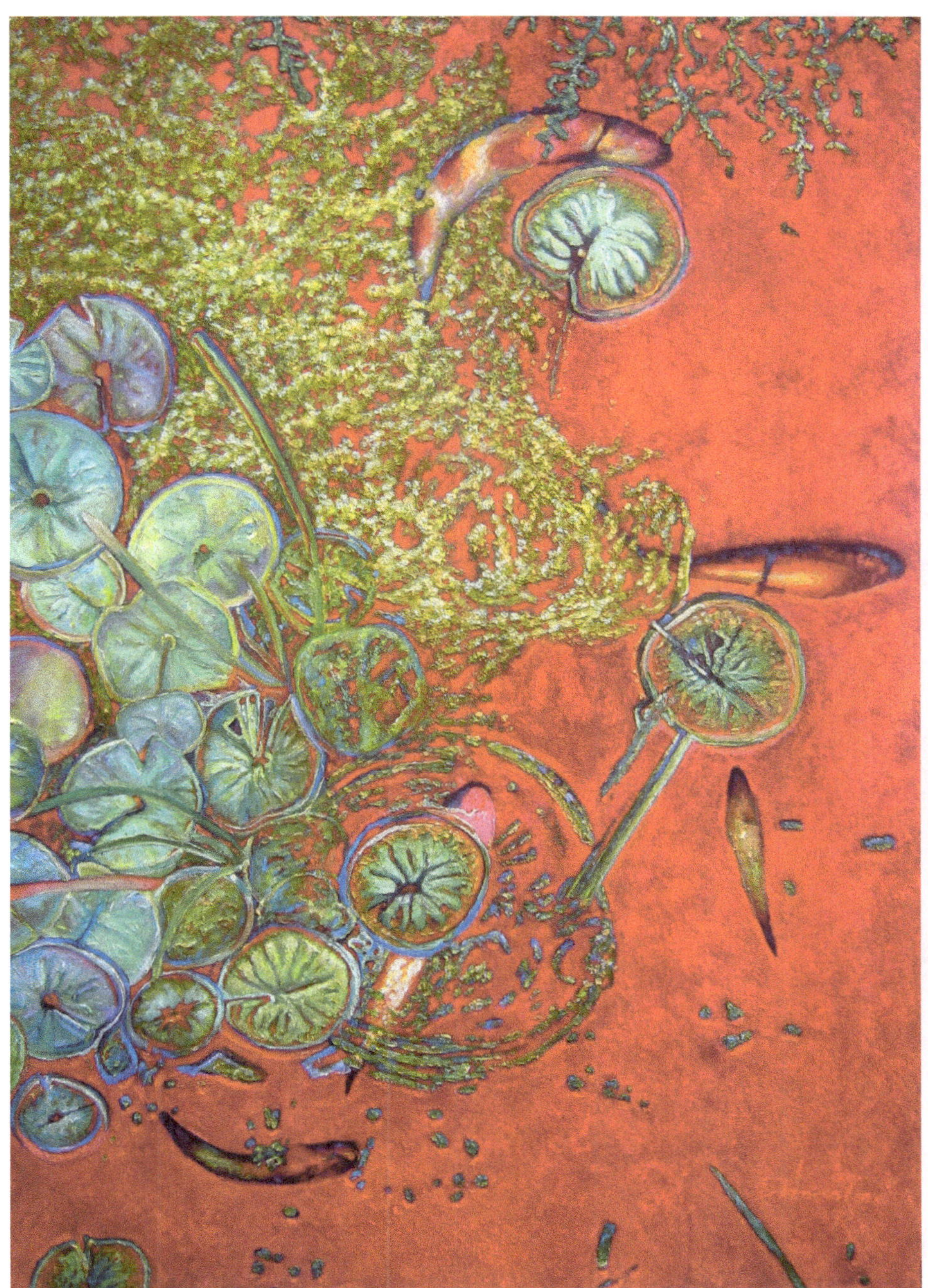

On Golden Pond

Dragon Attacking Elephant

The Dragon Mother
and the Azure Dragon Rising

David Hansford

The HillHelen Group LLC
127 Fairmont Ave., Jackson, TN 38301
hillhelengroup@gmail.com

Morning Light

To my wife, Laura
Who never wavered in her support and confidence in this endeavor,
And who herself personally knows of The Dragon Mother.

And to my sons, Wolff and Adam
With my hope that this story will have meaning to them
As they continue their life's journey.

Dog Berry

And a special thank you to Ann and Amy,
Who started all of this with me forty years ago.

Totems Along the Yellow River

Contents

Blue Moon

Paintings

Jacque's Sky

Introduction
The Spiritual Force

C. L. Nash, Songster

he spiritual force has always existed in this world, its ethereal presence wrapping itself around all life like the formless wind. As the capricious movement of the wind cannot be seen but is felt, the elemental nature of the spiritual force is illusive, but profoundly affects everything. Like the power of the wind, this force can be subtle, endowing blessings invigorating to all life, or it can be fierce, drastically altering or destroying that which it embraces.

The spiritual force is formed when primordial forces of creativity, magic, and love interact, moving through and binding the universe as vibrational frequencies. Through the vibrational frequencies, the universe is put into motion, animated as a dynamic, living whole. This includes the energetic forces and the material world, but not just these are in vibration. Emotions, beliefs, ideas, intentions, and actions — the un-things that define human existence — elicit vibrations, too. Every vibration has its own rhythm. Rhythms act upon one another and can be put into rhythmical relation, synchronizing to enhance, modify, or dampen each other.

The rhythms of creativity, magic, and love, being primordial, synchronize with the rhythms of the primal elements of fire, water, earth, and air, and all of these can synchronize with the rhythms of individuals, causing a power to come into play that shifts and alters perceptual reality. The creative rhythm, in conjunction with the magical rhythm, gives the altered reality shape and form. If guided by the rhythm of love, then the new reality will be beneficial to all life.

In the distant past, the sages and the shamans, as the tribe's wise ones, understood the visible world must be in harmony with the unseen one, and blended the magic and creative forces to connect the tribe's realities with the unseen forces influencing it. Whether in the dark recesses of a cave making drawings on the stone walls to appease the Great Bear Spirit for food, dancing in ceremonial patterns to the cadence of drums beseeching ancestors for protection from evil spirits, or reciting stories of mythological importance to explain the tribe's creation, the shamans and the sages ensured the tribe's survival.

Drawings, dances, music, stories — all to invoke the magic to keep the tribe alive. Magic was understood. Magic was embraced. Magic was real. Nothing has changed over the millennia; the survival of society as the expanded tribe is still at stake. The stewards of this magic are the creative ones — artists, musicians, poets, dancers, and the artists of life, for they are the shamans and sages of today. As it was for the wise ones of the past, it is their mission to embrace the magic to put the visible world into harmony with the unseen one. The magical energy embedded in the world synchronizes with the creative energy of the artist; these energies flow into a rhythmical relation, heightening the imagination with vitality, as from an unseen power. Artists are not isolated beings. By sharing their cosmically enhanced, creative rhythms with others and the world, the rhythm of life reveals itself to all in its most perfect expression.

In its most perfect expression, all life is intimately connected. People realize that they are not isolated beings and achieve beautiful relations not just with other human beings, but with the whole of life. The primordial magical rhythm enhances the creative rhythms, such that the intimate kinship between people's lives and the lives of animals, birds, trees, and plants is genuinely felt. A connection is deeply felt not just with other life, but with the whole of creation. The rhythms of wind, water, earth, and fire merge with individuals' rhythms, generating a sense of wholeness, balance, and harmony out of which emerges a profound sense of the beauty and wonder of the universe. The entire universe becomes the spiritual home to human beings, and with this a freedom is manifested, such that the survival of the tribe is assured, for only then is perfect love possible.

This is all ancient wisdom, forgotten in humankind's incessant obsession with ego, desire, and fear. How am I aware of this wisdom? The story that follows describes my journey toward spiritual understanding, a journey so fantastical that it will be difficult to believe. For the few who can see the truth in the implausible, the rewards are enormous. The mind must be swept clear of prejudice that only allows for standard conventions of thought and beliefs to savor the essence of the spiritual force, a blending of the rhythms of magic, creativity, and love. If you can do this, then perhaps you will believe me when I tell you that magic is real, dragons have always existed, and I have met the Dragon Mother.

Flight to Michoâcan

1

Ka'Mi, 'The Little Monkey'

Haiku by Basho

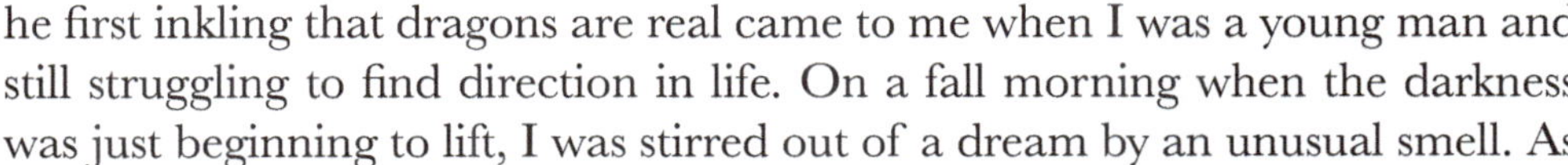

The first inkling that dragons are real came to me when I was a young man and still struggling to find direction in life. On a fall morning when the darkness was just beginning to lift, I was stirred out of a dream by an unusual smell. As always, the window at my head was open slightly to allow in the soothing night air, but this time it carried an odd odor. Not conscious, but also not asleep, I tried to think about the source of that peculiar scent, but my mind was unable to hold a focused thought. That was when the story of Ka'Mi crashed in on me, a vision that startled me out of my dreamy state and into clarity.

In a time long past, a young girl named Ka'Mi lived in a small village nestled in a glen and surrounded by tall trees of cedar and ginkgo. She was a happy child with honey-colored skin, black short-cropped, elflock hair, and a highly inquisitive nature that earned her the nickname "the little monkey."

It was the end of the dry season, and the grasslands on the encircling hills were brown and dry. The stream running through the glen was reduced to a trickle but provided enough water to green the trees and plants along the streamside. The people of the village waited in anticipation for the spring rains from the east that were overdue.

The villagers were hard-working folk who lived in harmony with the life around them. Many of them made a living by harvesting the odd-smelling seeds of the ginkgo trees to sell to the surrounding villages for use as medicines. The trees in the village were enormous, a blessing from antiquity. The rainy season was seldom late, so the tardiness of the rains caused anxiety among the people — except the little monkey, Ka'Mi, for she delighted in exploring the mysteries of nature.

Ka'Mi was playing at the village's edge, where a small clover patch, seeking moisture for its blossoms, grew along the stream's bank. She constructed a clover chain while singing to the bees buzzing excitedly around the flowers. At noontime, Ka'Mi wrapped the clover chain around her neck and skipped up the path to her home. Rounding an old barn, she came upon a well not used for many years. She was not sure if any water would be found in this abandoned well, especially now without the rains, but she was thirsty, so she walked over to the cedar pail perched on the circular stone base.

She stopped and caught her breath. The stone base was so decrepit that it leaned slightly, with stones dislodged here and there, forming small, shaded niches for tiny black beetles to escape the sun. Some stones of the base were cracked and chipped, with stains from the reddish-black soil creating an intricate pattern around the base. The wooden slats of the pail were warped and streaked with various shades of gray, and the rope binding it together was rotted and frayed along its length. The well was rough, deteriorating, and perfect in its imperfection! To Ka'Mi, the melancholy she felt emanating from the ancient well was serene beauty.

She started to pick up the pail when she noticed that twining tendrils of a morning glory plant, struggling among the stones, had wrapped around the pail's handle. On one tendril was a single blue flower, a glorious effort by the plant to fulfill its nature. Ka'Mi realized that she would have to break the tendril before attempting to find water. A large butterfly the color of fire lit on the blossom, then quickly flittered away.

Ka'Mi smiled. Admiring the tendril with its flower, she hummed a cheerful song, while gently touching the blue blossom. Removing the clover chain from her neck, she hung it on the water pail. Even with her thirst she chose not to disturb the blue flower's delicate beauty on its vine.

As Ka'Mi turned away from the well, a melodious jingling filled the air. She spun around, looking for its source, when a whirlwind of dust lifted from the well. As the spinning wind spiraled upward, it grew in intensity and size, slowly moving toward her. Workers among the ginkgo trees by the stream shrieked at Ka'Mi to run, but the little monkey was too fascinated. The wind funnel wrapped around her like a spinning chimney, and as she looked up into the expanding vortex, she glimpsed flashes of lustrous blue. As quickly as it started, the whirlwind dissipated, and there suspended in the clear sky was a terrifying, azure dragon, glaring down.

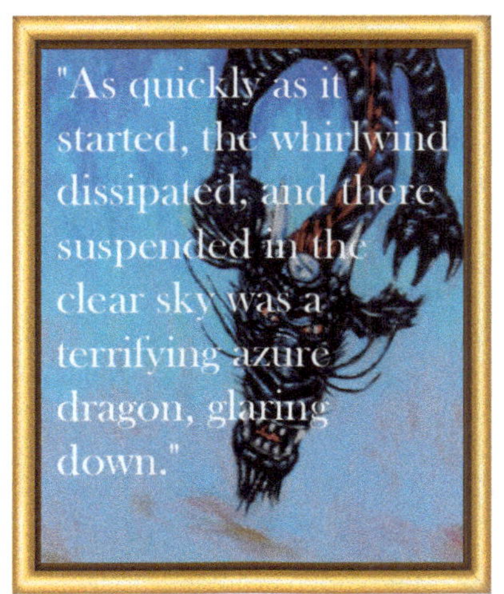

Its scowling head, with a flowing beard, straight horns, and glowing, fierce eyes, sat atop a long, serpentine body covered in blue scales and crested with bristling spines down its back. Four powerful, clawed limbs were embellished with flames of five colors. Ka'Mi whooped for joy. The dragon was ferocious and magnificent. Her excitement was so great that she felt no fear as the dragon looked down, and through its gaping mouth exhaled a soft, diaphanous veil of rain upon the girl — a benevolent gift for Ka'Mi's caring respect for the blue flower. The workers watched in stunned silence, for they realized that the little monkey had just received the dragon's blessing.

The dragon turned away and churned upward into the sky, all the while breathing out voluminous clouds, until the dragon disappeared in the dense haze. The clouds remained, but the azure dragon was gone. The workers spread the news of Ka'Mi and the dragon to the entire village. That night, the full moon, shining over the ginkgo tree's fluttering leaves, was encircled in a dazzling halo. Everyone knew what that meant — the rains were coming. The next day the nourishing rainy season began.

Ka'Mi lived her long life in the village. The moniker of "little monkey" stayed with her, for she never lost her love and joy in exploring the miraculous workings of nature; and for as long as she lived, the village was blessed with abundant, fertilizing rain.

Blue Bayou

2

Reflections on Painting

"I look beyond;
Flowers are not,
Nor tinted leaves.
On the sea beach
A solitary cottage stands
In the waning light
Of an autumn eve."

Sen no Rikyu

hy I had the vision of Ka'Mi was baffling, but its significance I understood. Ka'Mi's life was her passion; her existence gave her pleasure. Lofty ideals and daily burdens were of no consequence compared to her joy of being fully engaged with the world's vitality. Ka'Mi's life was blissful and free. The azure dragon in the vision was puzzling, but I was sure that I wanted that kind of life — a life where every day I awaken excited by its creative possibilities.

One drawing was all it took. A friend's birthday approached, and I thought to make a drawing for her. Over the course of two weeks, I stole from my studies whatever minutes I could to put pencil to paper. The enjoyment felt in executing that drawing of a little boy on a rickety, wooden porch was intoxicating. Drawing was always natural for me, so I should have realized that creativity was my purpose in life. I enrolled in art school.

Of course, my parents were chagrined at my decision to leave law school for a questionable career in the arts. I understood their concern, but when Dad challenged the value of art, I answered him with a question. If the arts have no intrinsic value, then why have authoritarian regimes always sought to control the artists? Dad did not respond, but I knew the answer. Artists in all fields seek to reveal truths. To do so, they jealously guard their freedom and independence. For those driven to control others, a freed mind is a problem.

After art school, enticed by the splendor of the ocean, I moved to a small beach town for the serenity to paint. The town was a close-knit and friendly community. The houses were of the old, beachy type — wood frame, shingles, big sash windows to enjoy the ocean breezes, and wide overhanging eaves as protection from the sun. A short walk up the white sand beach was an area left to nature, where towering dunes, wrapped in sea oats, absorbed the power of the surging waves.

It became my habit to walk to these dunes at sunrise, and again when the sun was low behind the barrier island. There was a dreamy quality to these transitional times, especially in the evening, when the sky glowed yellow and orange, streaked with clouds of violet and gray, while the ocean reflected a peaceful, silvery green, conducive to contemplation. I sat regularly at the dunes, allowing the crashes of the breaking waves to lull me into quiet. These times of meditation on the beach became an essential part of my everyday life.

The studio was in the sunroom of my small beach cottage. I painted off and on during the day and evening, breaking frequently to keep eyes and mind fresh. Painting was most productive after the walks on the beach. I felt charged with creative energy at these times; ideas and solutions came freely. While painting, I had clearer insights into the creative process. In art school, traditional principles were taught, but after years of painting, I ceased my reliance on principles, for I operated with a more holistic view of the life in each painting. Principles were not abandoned; they were internalized, flowing with the conscious and subconscious act of painting. Originally, my painting was rooted in the notion that art was an imitation of nature, of the physical appearance of things. As the insight into the creative process matured, I realized that the unseen acting on the seen, that is, the forces acting upon the material, caused patterns to emerge. To envision the forces, I observed the patterns. By focusing on the rhythmic nature of the patterns, a different quality was infused into the paintings, one that hinted at the workings of nature.

The canopies of trees were a dominant subject matter. I concentrated on the patterns the leaves and branches wove as they intertwined, and on the asymmetrical balance that always seemed present in a matured tree. At some point, instead of looking up into the trees for subject matter, I looked down, studying the rhythms and patterns on the ground, on the beach sand, and ultimately down upon pond water. Here is when my perception of reality began to wobble. While I painted one of the many variations on ponds, the inward voice that typically mused while I painted shifted to a different intonation. Words formed in my mind, but they had a soft undertone to them, like coins jingling together. It was not the same monkey-mind conversation I was accustomed to carrying on with myself. Another voice was inserting itself into my private, internal conversation.

As I kept painting the pond, the voice intoned, "Paint what you know; paint what you want to know. Paint water as it flows, the music it makes, as it ripples over stones, soothing, uplifting, mesmerizing. Paint water still as a quiet pond, solid, immutable, and mysterious, reflecting all in its mirrored surface. Paint water as a primal power, formless, adapting, accommodating, never the same, never finished. Paint water as the ultimate symbol of life."

At first, I was confused, but I attempted to paint as the voice said. The patterns and rhythms in the pond twisted and shifted with distractions, distortions, and dissolutions, until it revealed itself as something very different. When I finished and sat back to consider the image before me, the jingling voice said: "The painter becomes what he paints."

Over the next few months, I continued to paint ponds. The strange voice did not speak again, but I reflected often on the last statement. My meditation progressed, the incessant chatter in my mind controlled by using the ocean sounds as a mantra to soothe body and mind. I felt a greater sense of well-being and peace; nevertheless, my world view was about to be forever shaken, because the time was approaching for me to meet the Dragon Mother.

Black Stones

3

Meditating With Wordsworth

"The World is too much with us; late and soon,
Getting and spending, we lay waste our powers;
Little we see in Nature that is ours;
We have given our hearts away, a sordid boon!
This sea that bares her bosom to the moon;
The winds that will be howling at all hours,
And are up-gathered now like sleeping flowers;
For this, for everything, we are out of tune;
It moves us not. — Great God! I'd rather be
A Pagan suckled in a creed outworn,
So might I, standing on this pleasant lea,
Have glimpses that would make me less forlorn;
Have sight of Proteus rising from the sea,
Or hear old Triton blow his wreathed horn."

"The World Is Too Much With Us,"
William Wordsworth

When I was a young man, I discovered this sonnet by Wordsworth in a little book of poems. It was the first four lines that resonated with me, as I understood this to be a criticism of society dominated by the idea that humankind was lord of the earth and the center of the universe. The rest of nature existed only to satisfy people's needs and desires, for the primacy of life was devotion to making money and obtaining things. People were above and separate from the rest of life in the world. This disturbing disconnect with other life and the creation resonated deeply within me, for I could see that it resulted in a spiritual disconnect. If the majesty and mystery of the creation were shunned and abused, then how does that demonstrate love and awe toward the Creator? I was extremely discomforted by this realization.

Not long after discovering Wordsworth's sonnet, I was discussing the poem with a history professor friend, Dr. Leo, when on a lark I asked what in his extensive studies had the most significance for him. He answered without hesitation: "The history of humankind is the constant struggle to be free." Then he added: "Avoid like the plague people of money and power." Wordsworth would have approved of that, I thought.

"What does it mean to be free?" I asked him.

Dr. Leo smiled, "Yes, that is the crucial question. There is only one true freedom — freedom of the mind. Regardless of your situation in life, if your mind is free, then you have freedom. All other notions of freedom are an illusion."

Many years later I rediscovered the poem, while meandering in my library — the little book of poems tucked between two large art books, Noguchi and Klee. It was a joy to read the poem again, and as I had memorized the poem years ago, rereading it brought it all back.

Later that evening I decided to recite the poem as a mantra during a meditation session. My bed was in the corner between two sash windows. Both windows were open, allowing a pleasant ocean breeze to flutter the gossamer curtains. Propping the pillows on the bed, I crossed my legs, closed my eyes, and began to slowly recite the poem. My breathing was measured, interposed by little pauses. Naturally, random thoughts drifted in, but they were released immediately. Little by little, the pulsing of the blood rocked my body into relaxation. My breath softened to a thin wisp — air barely moving. External awareness faded with only the soothing rhythms within remaining.

Suddenly, a tingling sensation jolted me out of the calm. As it subsided, my internal awareness shifted to an unusual setting around me. It was as if I were in a Chinese landscape painting. There was emptiness, the space vast and indistinct, but with far-distant mountains retreating into mist. On the mountains were hints of pine trees and waterfalls. Clouds languidly drifted here and there, dissolving into rain and then re-forming. The horizon flowed lazily all around me, varying in depth and distance, like seeking infinity but not finding it. It was a dreamlike landscape that did not feel like a physical place.

Out of the mist materialized a woman atop a magnificent beast of some kind, or was the beast part of her? I was not sure. A golden, diaphanous robe was wrapped elegantly about her; curly, raven hair spilled down her back. She was a mature woman, who echoed youthful beauty, her gilded skin glistening with an inner fire. The creature she appeared perched upon glowed golden as well, but it was so large that its limits were enshrouded in swirling clouds.

"Out of the mist materialized a woman atop a magnificent beast of some kind, or was the beast part of her?"

Floating in the air before the woman was a lotus flower. The flower glowed also, but of a cool blue that gleamed a green halo in the golden light of the beast. Without releasing her look on the lotus flower, the woman said, "Hello, David, it is time that we met."

Her voice! I recognized the voice. It was the jingling-jangling voice I had heard in my head months ago, but her actual voice had a wonderful, melodious quality. Its cheerful, bright tone was rich with an edginess that was both exciting and soothing.

"I was meditating in my bedroom," I stammered. "I am not sure where I am. Am I in a dream, or is this another vision?"

Still gazing at her flower, she replied, "Ah, yes ... well, a dream? No. I am not part of any dream. A vision — perhaps. I brought you here, David."

She never stopped looking at the flower, and by this point my attention was focused on the lotus flower, too. "Why are you staring at the flower?" I asked.

"I am not staring at the lotus flower. I am contemplating the lotus flower. A very different intent."

I suppose I looked confused, so she continued. "The lotus is a means of intense concentration; by understanding the essence of this flower, I gain a profound understanding of the universal, and through the universal, I get a glimpse of infinity, and with that glimpse I obtain a mind freed and become one with the spiritual rhythm that empowers all in the universe."

"You discovered all that from staring at a flower?" I asked incredulously.

"Oh, much more than that, David, and again, I was not staring. Here, focus on this lotus flower and see what truths might come to you."

With her eyes she directed the flower over to me until it floated in front of my face. "Now sweep your mind clear of thoughts and feelings on everything but the lotus. Become neutral. When you get that, let go of the appearance of the flower, and concentrate on the process of becoming a lotus flower. Finally, synchronize the rhythms of your mind and body with the rhythms inherent in the flower that define its making."

It seemed impossible, but I attempted to do as the golden woman said. As I focused on the flower, my breathing began to slow into a gentle rhythm. I could feel my heartbeat lose intensity until it was barely beating. My eyes, intensely upon the lotus flower, slowly closed until they were only slits, and my vision relaxed as the flower blurred. I do not know how long I meditated on the lotus, but suddenly, my eyes snapped open as a realization popped into my head, and I cried out, "Life lost!"

I looked over at the golden woman, who was studying me. "Very interesting," she whispered. "Please explain."

"The lotus flower has been plucked," I exclaimed. "It is not connected to its source of life, to its plant and the roots and the water in which it grew. This flower is a dying object. Its beauty is fading for it is no longer a living thing. To look at the flower, it appears beautiful, but it is rapidly transforming into a dried-out husk." In puzzling over what I had just rattled off, I was struck by the irony that plucked flowers are given as symbols of love. Perhaps, more appropriate as symbols of love lost.

The lotus flower floating before me faded away, as the golden woman continued my line of thought. "Very good, David. The flower's true beauty is not in its appearance, but in its connection to the rhythmical movement of all life. Yes, the physical presence of the lotus flower, its symmetry, balance, and color, can delight the senses and give joy, but it is the rhythm of life the whole plant possesses joined with the rhythm of all of life that reveals its true beauty."

Studying me, she added, "In the same way, if people are not connected to their source of life, are not they also becoming dried-up husks?"

It was a rhetorical question, I knew, and as I looked around, anxiety gripped me, for the bizarreness of the situation finally registered. "Where am I, and what is happening?"

"David, your body is on the bed in a deep meditative state. I joined with your life rhythms and brought you here to the In-Between, a transitional reality between the forces of the universe and the physical aspect of the universe. Your creative rhythm is resonating with increasing intensity and has attracted the magical rhythm, and with your daily meditative practice, you are on the path to enlightenment and transformation. The In-Between and I can help you on this journey."

The anxiety did not lessen, but I listened carefully as she continued. "You are here because it was time for you to be aware of here." After a slight pause she added, "Besides, you were reciting Wordsworth and that intrigued me.

"Now, control your mind and cleanse the fears. I have a story to tell you, but first, I want to ask you about the Wordsworth poem you were reciting. Tell me your thoughts about this part:

> *'... This sea that bares her bosom to the moon;*
> *The winds that will be howling at all hours,*
> *And are up-gathered now like sleeping flowers;*
> *For this, for everything, we are out of tune;*
> *It moves us not. — Great God! I'd rather be*
> *A Pagan suckled in a creed outworn,*
> *So might I, standing on this pleasant lea,*
> *Have glimpses that would make me less forlorn;*
> *Have sight of Proteus rising from the sea,*
> *Or hear old Triton blow his wreathed horn.' "*

Feeling more relaxed and enjoying the conversation with this fascinating woman, I answered, "The first part of the poem struck a more relevant chord with me; on the other hand, I enjoyed the imagery of this last part of the sonnet. It seemed like a longing on Wordsworth's part for a simpler time, where one lived more in harmony with nature."

"Yes, there is that, but that is not all," she responded. "Wordsworth was yearning for the dragons."

Totally confused now, I cried out, "What?"

"William spent time in the In-Between, for he was quite fond of the peacefulness here. He liked to contemplate upon the beauty of the waterfalls that you see in the distance."

She recited then what I assumed to be another Wordsworth poem:

" *A small Cascade fresh swoln with snows*
Thus threatened a poor Briar-rose,
That, all bespattered with his foam,
And dancing high and dancing low,
Was living, as a child might know,
In an unhappy home.' "

I reacted, "That is a disturbing poem to be the contemplation of a beautiful waterfall."

"Yes, well, William embraced the tranquility that exists in the In-Between to contemplate human feelings with the bonds with nature, in his effort of self-realization — his search to free his mind. After all, David, is that not the function of the artist and the poet?

"As you noticed, William was instilled with an ingrained sadness that shaded his joy of a spiritual life with nature. The sorrows of humankind overwhelmed him. Ultimately, he declined the path to transformation."

The golden woman quoted again.

" *'There was a time when meadow, grove, and stream,*
The earth, and every common sight,
To me did seem
Apparelled in celestial light,
The glory and the freshness of a dream.
It is not now as it hath been of yore; —
Turn wheresoe'er I may,

By night or day,
The things which I have seen I now can see no more.'

"The melancholy and despair in this poem is heart-rending, for he saw the relation of humankind to the rest of creation as imperfect. I fear that he did not grasp the truth that although the lives of people are imperfect, impermanent, and incomplete; nonetheless, they are constantly in a dynamic flow and capable of resonating with the primordial rhythms, thus touching perfection, even if just for a moment.

"While here, William did enjoy his conversations with Li-Dan. They spent much time together in philosophical conversations. Li-Dan spoke to William of old truths — truths from very early in this Age — and William hinted at those truths when he wrote of 'Proteus,' " she continued. "Do you know of Proteus?"

"Not really, I think he was a Greek god of some kind, associated with water. But ... but I don't understand. Wordsworth was here? How is that possible? You called him William; you knew him? And who is Li-Dan?"

She smiled and replied, "So many questions. He came here the same way you did, and for the same reason, and yes, I knew him well. David, I have been here for a long time. But that is not a story for now. Li-Dan is better known by his noble title of Lao Tzu, the Old Master. But let's return to Proteus.

"Proteus was an ancient Greek god of the sea, rivers, and other bodies of water. As such, he embodied the idea of change, as is the nature of water. Proteus portended future events, foretold momentous changes, and he could assume many forms at will. Proteus was the ancient Greeks' tendril of a memory for the original god of the sea and water; the same tendril that has twisted its way down through every civilization since the beginning of this Age — the original water god, the dragon.

"Now, if you are ready, I will tell you a story. I like a good story, for there is much to learn from them. This is a very old story, one of my favorites, called 'Hana's Promise.' "

Hana Washing Clothes

Hana Meeting Old Man

4

Hana's Promise

Tao Te Ching, Verse 3 by Lao Tzu

 long, long time ago in a land very far away, there lived a young girl by the name of Hana. Hana was a most beautiful child with a face that shone like the full moon and long, silky hair as black as the night. Her eyes sparkled like two little stars, and her lips were as delicate as rose petals. Never was there anyone as lovely as she. As beautiful as she was, her beauty did not compare with that of her heart, for it was filled with only kindness and love. Her gentle spirit reached out to touch the world around her. Her greatest joy was walking the forest path with nature's garden nestled among misty blue hills and streams murmuring their eternal song. Hana relished the rhythm of life that touched her and animated the world around her.

"Hana lived in a little town beside a river at the base of a tall hill. The river was deep and wide and could be crossed only at the town, where the water was shallow. The town was on a trade route between East and West, and every day, caravans of horses, camels, mules, and herds of cows stopped by the town to cross the river, either coming or going from exotic and faraway places. Therefore, the town became known as Cow Ford. There was much buying and selling, so the town of Cow Ford prospered and grew wealthy as the years passed. As the town gained in wealth, the people increasingly lost their benevolent nature. They no longer cared about anything except obtaining riches. Greed dominated the whole town, and everything in life existed only to satisfy their avarice. Mothers no longer cared for their children; husbands no longer loved their wives. The townspeople stopped greeting. In fact, no one would say 'good morning' unless they were first paid a silver coin.

"The townspeople were gluttonous for the finest of worldly goods, and so they became highly fearful for the safety of their gold and jewels, since nobody trusted anyone else. They built a high wall around the town for protection from outsiders; and every person built a smaller wall around their house and put locks upon the doors and bars upon the windows. Similarly, they constructed walls and locks in their minds, no longer feeling a continuity with all of creation; they became dark inside with no light of kinship with animals, trees, and plants, no reverence for the primal forces of life. Everyone in the town became like this — greedy, envious, fearful — all except Hana, who remained innocent and pure.

"Hana's mother and father were as selfish and greedy as anybody in Cow Ford, so they made little Hana work long hours to pay for her food and room. Every day before the sunlight touched the earth, Hana walked down to the riverbank where flat rocks served as the town laundry. There she washed the soiled clothes of the townspeople. As Hana scrubbed the clothes, she would sing as the fish in the river came to the surface to dance and leap. When the orange sun dropped low in the sky and gradually disappeared, Hana put aside her work and walked exhaustedly home. She was tired but cheerful, for she was happy and found joy in every day.

"Hana had a constant companion who followed her every day to work, a ragamuffin dog she called Gaea. The tattered dog showed up on the first day that Hana's parents decided Hana was old enough to earn money and put her to work doing laundry. The dog with her unkempt, bristly short hair, long nose, and pointy ears looked like a street dog, but her eyes of a brilliant golden yellow were piercing and aware and suggested more. Gaea was devoted to Hana and was never far from her. To anyone paying attention, it was clear she was Hana's protector. To Hana, Gaea was simply her best and only friend.

"One evening when the moon was full and peeping over the hill, Hana gathered her basket of clean clothes and started walking briskly down the road into town. Gaea trotted just behind her. She was walking along the main path to town when she came upon an exquisite spider web, glistening in the moonlight. Hana did not wish to disturb the spider's work, so she moved onto a little side path that eventually rejoined the main one. Rounding a bend, she was startled to see in the pale moonlight an old man standing under a tall ginkgo tree. Seldom did she come across someone during the evening walk. He quickly made a kindly gesture for her to come over and talk to him. Gaea ambled over to the old man. Hana relaxed and followed her.

"He was not much taller than Hana, with a body frail and bent, leaning heavily on a walking stick. Yet there was a strong, almost magical power in his eyes. They appeared to Hana to glow with a soft, eerie light, and with a hint of fire. He was wearing a white robe of the most exquisite cloth Hana had ever seen, so delicate she thought it could be pulled through the eye of a needle; and underneath his chin, behind a small wisp of a beard, was a large pearl of reddish hue hung on a silver chain.

"They talked for a while, and Hana was enchanted, for never had anyone been so kind and gentle with her. Suddenly, a torrential rain of huge drops fell upon them. It was a most peculiar rain, for Hana could see no clouds in the moonlit sky from whence it might have come. Hana was unconcerned, for she always found the rain a phenomenon of endless beauty, but the old man invited her into his humble house to wait out the storm, so she did. They sat down by the fire to dry out and drank small bowls of hot jasmine tea and talked quietly. As they talked, Hana felt very warm and contented and was growing ever fonder of this unusual old man.

"After a while, the storm was over, and Hana prepared to leave. She knew her parents would be angry if she did not quickly bring home the money she had made that day. Hana bowed and thanked the kindly old man, whereupon the old man said, 'Hana, I sense that your heart has a love for the life of the earth, the waters, and the wind. No one else in this town feels as you do. I have an important need, so I want to ask you if you will promise to render a service for me.'

"Being the gentle person that she was, and eager to repay his kindness, she quickly promised.

" 'I am going to die, sweet Hana,' he told her, 'before the full moon begins to wane. I have searched the town from the mighty to the lowly and you are the only honest and decent person to whom I can entrust this egg.'

"The old man handed her a silver egg, shaped like a hen's egg, but much larger. 'You must not let this egg out of the care of your arms for a whole year, until you can hear a jingling-jangling sound within the egg that causes the wind to stop and then rapidly rise. When this happens, you must go to the riverbank and cast the silver egg upon the waters. There is magic protecting the egg that will prevent anyone from taking it away from you against your will, and it will help you from tiring in holding it.'

"Great sadness came upon Hana's heart to hear that the old man was dying, for she had never known such kindness; and as two tears trickled down her cheeks, Hana gave the old man a forlorn smile, gathered the egg in the clothes basket, and started on her way home. Gaea gazed for a poignant moment into the eyes of the old man, who looked sadly back, then turned and accompanied Hana back to town.

"When Hana reached the town, she delivered the clean clothes, collected her money, and briskly walked home. Her parents were furious at her being late, but their curiosity about the large silver egg she was carrying tempered their anger. Hana told them the whole story about meeting the old man, and the promise she made.

"Malicious smiles slowly parted her parents' faces. 'That was very clever of you to make that promise to the foolish old man,' they said. 'Now give us the egg, for its size and value will increase our wealth tenfold.'

" 'No, I cannot,' cried Hana. 'I promised the old man I would hold it until I heard a jingling-jangling sound inside that causes the wind to stop and rapidly rise, and then I would cast it upon the waters of the river.'

"Her angry parents tried to take the egg out of Hana's arms, but they could not. Finally, in their frustration and anger, they threw her out of the house and onto the streets. Hana had become of no use to them; now with her arms holding the silver egg, she could no longer work and bring home money. Hana was distraught when she walked out the door of her house, but Gaea was patiently waiting for her. Gaea, the street dog, led Hana to a sheltered spot for the night, where Hana would be secure.

"The next morning began the first of many days that Hana sought work and a place to stay. But with the large silver egg in her arms, there was not much she could do. Besides, when people saw the egg, their only interest was in how they could procure it. No one could, and always Gaea was close by watching over Hana. In desperation the unfortunate girl was forced to beg from door to door and to sleep out in the open, with little shelter from the cold, rain, and wind. The people in Cow Ford were so selfish and greedy that whenever she asked for a small morsel of food, she received the same answer: 'Give me that beautiful silver egg, little Hana, and I will give you something to eat and a bed to sleep in.'

"And always Hana answered, 'No, I cannot. I promised the old man I would hold it until I heard a jingling-jangling sound inside as the wind stops and rapidly rises, and then cast it upon the waters of the river.'

"Everybody in Cow Ford tried to take the silver egg away from Hana, but none could, so they pushed her away, treated her harshly, and gave her no comfort. No one in their greed and desires would help Hana; not even the priest offered sanctuary. Everyone in the town soon realized that no one could obtain the valuable egg, so she became an outcast. The year passed, and it was a year of ridicule and abuse. Always Gaea protected her, found shelter that offered a little protection, and somehow, Gaea always brought tiny scraps of food for Hana to eat. Still, Hana grew thin and weak, yet because of her gentle nature, she accepted her plight in silence, and still tried to find some joy in each day. And neither did she let go of the egg — not for one moment — for she had promised the old man.

"As the year came to an end, Hana was barely alive. She lived only to fulfill her promise to the old man. One day, she was slowly shuffling along the main street of the town, murmuring a soft song to Gaea, when suddenly she heard a jingling-jangling sound within the silver egg. Hana held her breath, her heart beating rapidly, and listened again. Once more, she heard the jingling-jangling sound, when the wind abruptly stopped blowing and then began to furiously rise straight up. Hana stumbled to the bank of the river as fast as her emaciated little body would take her. Gaea was right beside her, and with the last bit of strength Hana had left, she threw the silver egg out upon the water.

"The shell immediately began to dissolve, the silver coating the surface of the water until there remained only an ugly lump of flesh floating on the silvery, shining surface of the river. As Hana looked upon this in astonishment, the lump began to quiver, and then it began to grow and change. It contracted and expanded, over and over, growing larger and larger, until finally it transformed into an enormous white dragon, floating on the water. Its dazzling body, covered with glowing scales, was so long Hana could barely see its end. Running down the dragon's back were spines like flickering flames, and on its head were two silver horns. Its scowling face was both ferocious and royal with eyes like fierce balls of fire. And under its chin behind a small wisp of a beard, Hana could see a large pearl of reddish hue. The dragon moved toward Hana as if it wished to speak to her. Hana's heart was about to burst with happiness, for never had she seen anything as magnificent and grand as that white dragon. But being so weak from her sufferings, all Hana could do was smile tearfully at the dragon as she fell softly to the ground, lifeless.

"The white dragon reared its head back in a fury and roared into the sky with a deafening, clanging-banging scream that trembled the earth below. Everyone in Cow Ford, hearing the roar and feeling the maelstrom building in the sky, ran panic-stricken down to the river. Watching in horror, they saw the tremendous, terrifying white beast churning round and round, climbing upward in the sky. Loud cracks of thunder hurled the people of Cow Ford to the ground as huge bolts of lightning tore down from clouds that blackened the sky.

"The dragon whipped the winds into hurricane force, while vomiting torrential rain and fireballs down upon the town. The men of Cow Ford hid their faces, while the children screamed with fear. The walls crumbled, homes burned, and all traces of wealth washed away. As the storm abated, the magnificent white dragon soared to the summit of the hill above the river, and, casting a last glance down at Hana, rose higher and higher until it disappeared into the clouds above.

"The people who were left picked themselves out of the rubble and rushed to the bank of the river, there to see poor Hana lying dead. They were amazed; she seemed more beautiful than ever before, her smiling face shining like the full moon. Sorry for their wicked ways of greed and selfishness, and their abuse of such a kind and gentle child, the people began to wail loudly and weep, rolling upon the ground. They tore their clothes and pulled their hair, for so great was their grief and misgivings.

"Hana's mother and father had the greatest sorrow as they had mistreated their own daughter, who had shown them only love. Her mother and father carried Hana to the waters of the river and bathed her and brushed out her long, silky black hair. All the people took Hana to the foot of the hill and laid her carefully on the bank by the flat rocks, promising upon her peaceful body that they would never again return to their wicked and greedy ways. Off to the side, scrutinizing the repentant townspeople with piercing, brilliant golden eyes was Gaea, the street dog. If anyone had been watching the dog, they would have seen her gradually disappear into a cloudy mist — a mist that floated over to Hana's body and tenderly raised her from the riverbank. Higher and higher, Hana rose on the mist until she, too, disappeared in the clouds above.

"The townspeople of Cow Ford did not have time to be in wonder of Hana's rising, for just then, pearls the size of carriage wheels fell from the sky, covering Hana's resting place. In the middle of the pearls, a huge ginkgo tree sprang up with silver leaves that fluttered in the breeze like sparkling butterflies. Around the pearls grew thick vines of white roses that bloom all year. Everybody smiled at the grandeur of it, for never was there anything on earth more beautiful than this. From that time on, the river was known as the Silver River, the hill was known as the Dragon's Peak, and the town, a kind and happy place, was forevermore called Hana's Ford.

"As the years passed, when the people from Hana's Ford looked up on a cloudy day, they were certain that they glimpsed Hana smiling down upon them, and when the breeze began to blow, they knew they heard her gentle voice singing. On such days, people would say, 'It is a Hana Blessed Day.' "

While the golden woman told the story, she had a faraway expression with a small smile, as if recalling a tender memory. Finishing the tale, she turned her attention toward me, and she asked, "Well, did you like Hana's story?"

I replied honestly, "Yes, I did, but I did not understand; did Hana really die? And Gaea, the dog, was mysterious. What was she?"

The golden woman smiled. "Mysterious, yes, I suppose so. There are more stories for you; then you will understand. As for Hana, she transformed. Before you ask the obvious question, it is time for you to leave. Soon you will have the opportunity to meet Li-Dan. I think you will find that most illuminating, but for now, please put yourself back into a meditative state and return to your bed. It has been a pleasure to talk with you. We will meet again before too long, David."

"Wait," I shouted. "I do not know who you are. What is your name?"

She answered simply, "I am the Dragon Mother."

Dragon Attacking Cow

Dragon as an Old Man

5
Discourses With a Fish

Tao Te Ching, Verse 10, Lao Tzu

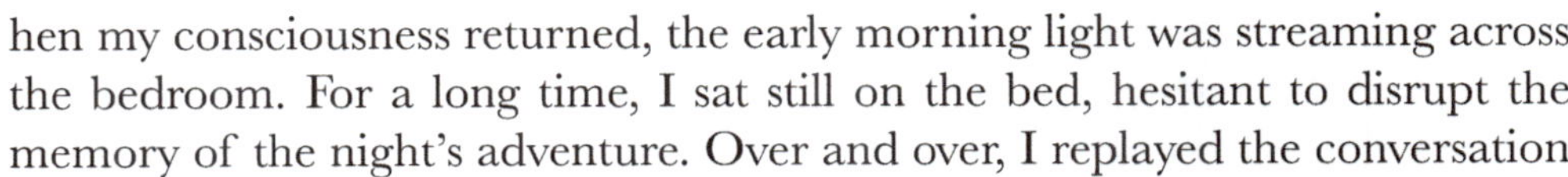

hen my consciousness returned, the early morning light was streaming across the bedroom. For a long time, I sat still on the bed, hesitant to disrupt the memory of the night's adventure. Over and over, I replayed the conversation with the Dragon Mother, trying to make sure I did not miss any nuance of the revelations revealed to me. Foremost in my mind was the existence of the In-Between, which I did not understand, and there was the question as to why the Dragon Mother told me the story ... and what is a Dragon Mother? And, oh yes, the crazy idea that DRAGONS ARE REAL!

After breakfast, I walked up the beach to my meditation spot, secluded by a tall, primary dune and the wildness behind. The Dragon Mother had told me that soon I would meet Li-Dan, but the morning was uninterrupted. After an hour of meditation, I strolled leisurely home, walking along the strand where the incoming tide rolled over dry sand, creating little pockets of trapped air. I called them "sand bubbles" and for some reason enjoyed popping them with my toes as I walked. Silly, I know. Strange how the simplest of activities can give joy.

As I walked, the tide came in and out, arranging and rearranging the scattered shells along the beach. Shells of different sizes and shapes, some turned up and some turned down, appeared to be scattered randomly, but after walking awhile, I began to see that the tide was ordering the shells in the randomness. Arriving at home, I immediately headed into the studio, pulled out a canvas, and began to build a painting that captured the ebb and flow of the water upon the shells.

The painting session that day was a good one, finishing in the late afternoon. The sun was turning orange as it dropped low behind the island's marsh side. This was my favorite time to be along the ocean, when the changing light in the sky reflected silvery green on the water. Flights of pelicans glided in formation to their evening resting places. Sanderlings skittered in the retreating surf's thin film, legs a blur, stopping abruptly to stick their little beaks into the sand, hoping for a tiny morsel. And every now and then, there was the cackling cry of the laughing gull, "haah-ha-ha-ha-haaah," flying overhead. It was a glorious time to be trekking back for an evening meditation.

The island I lived on was a barrier island, formed of sediment and sand, worked and reworked by wind-driven waves until land was formed with sand dunes piled up on the ocean side and reed marshes and muck flourishing on the land side. The mounded dunes were driven to heights by the wind's ceaseless energy and were topped with the sea oats' swaying, golden stalks, a natural haven for quiet meditation. My favorite dune reminded me of a turtle, a big humped dune as the shell and then tapering down to a smaller dune for the head — my "turtle dune," a special place to go peacefully inward.

I settled into my seated pose, but I could not close my eyes. The moon was full and recently risen over the ocean, moonlight rippling and bouncing off every movement of the waves, creating a mesmerizing light show. As I focused on the flickering lights, my breathing slowed, and serenity permeated mind and body. That was when something peculiar happened. My eyes were fixed placidly on the light playing upon the water, when a strange mist appeared. Materializing off the water, it gradually obscured the moonlight as it moved toward me. I suppose I should have been unnerved, but given the strangeness I had already experienced at the In-Between, I sat quietly and waited. As the mist embraced me in a comforting caress, I closed my eyes and slowed my breathing to a thin wisp. I was moving into a deep meditative state when I heard in a low-pitched, clinging-clanging voice, "Greetings, David."

Opening my eyes, I was quite astonished to see a large fish head poking out of the water looking at me. Yes, it truly was a fish, scales glowing silver and red, a face with large, bulging fish eyes, and fish lips that looked as if they could form words, and they did!

"Are you gobsmacked to see me?"

"Gobsmacked? What?" I stammered.

"Astonished. I believe the Dragon Mother told you we would meet soon."

"You're Li-Dan?" I exclaimed. The fish bobbed his head in what I thought must be a fish nod. "The Dragon Mother did tell me, but she said you were Lao Tzu, the Old Master. She said nothing about you being a fish."

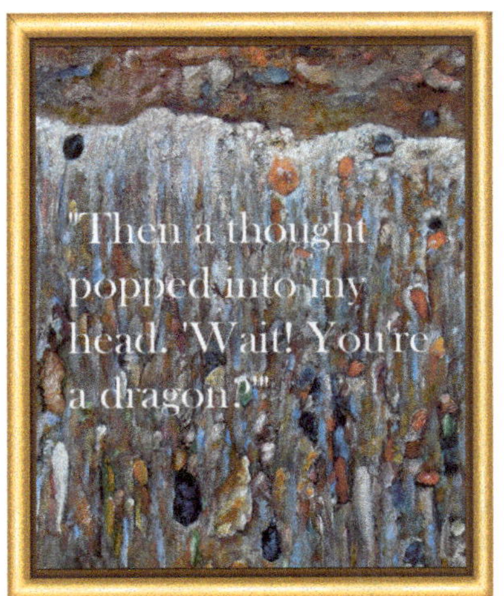

"Don't be bumfuzzled. Today, I am a fish. Tomorrow? I don't know. What do you think?" Or is this all tarradiddle to you?"

"Tarradiddle?" I was amused at his word choice. "You use odd-sounding words, and what do you mean about being something else tomorrow? That is quite a conundrum to me." I decided to try an odd-sounding word, too.

Li-Dan smiled bizarrely with his fish lips. "Good, good. Fun words are never used enough. What does it matter what form I assume, if my identity remains intact? Dragon transformations are unlimited. We have the power to cast off assumed forms. Over the centuries, humans have envisioned the most ridiculous countenances for dragons, the result of thinking dragons are mere fantasy. But consider this, David, if the primordial force of magic can synchronize with the primordial force of creativity, giving structure to an idea that can fuse with the material world, then why is the possibility of transforming into different forms such a cockamamie idea?"

Li-Dan the fish peered at me with those googly fish eyes. I really did not know how to answer that. He had lost me, so I said nothing and stared back into those googly eyes, radiating with such an intensity that it was difficult to look away. The mist still surrounded us, cloaking us in a private, surreal space. Then a thought popped into my head. "Wait! You're a dragon?"

He gave me a fish chuckle, which with the clinging-clanging tone was strange enough. "How else could I talk with you? Fish don't talk, David. The Dragon Mother sent me to tell you about dragons to prepare you for your next stage of awareness."

I considered that for a moment. "So the Dragon Mother is a dragon, too. When I was in the In-Between, I thought she was riding a beast, but the beast was her!"

"Well, of course, she is a dragon, and at another time, I will tell you the story of the Dragon Mother, but for now, understand that the Dragon Mother is not from this Age of Humankind."

"Age of Humankind? I don't know what that is," I said.

"Now is not the time for you to know, but the Dragon Mother has been here a very long time. As you saw in the In-Between, she is a golden-yellow dragon, THE golden-yellow dragon who taught the great Sage Fu Hsi about yin-yang."

Li-Dan saw my gawking expression, but he continued, "Don't be discombobulated, David. The Dragon Mother instructed Sage Fu Hsi on how duality forms the philosophical base to understand the structure and interactions of the universe. Yin-yang reveals the opposite nature that exists in all aspects of the universe, and between all aspects. The Dragon Mother revealed this to Sage Fu Hsi, and from him the knowledge was passed down from sage and shaman through thousands of years to benefit their tribes. Not just the reality of duality, but the absolute importance of balance within the complementary and opposing sides of duality. Maintaining the proper balance is the ultimate responsibility of the sages and shamans. The ever-shifting nature of that balance is the enigma that they must continually resolve, and they do so through their enlightened understanding. When the duality is in proper harmony, the happiness of the tribe is assured."

I was beginning to understand, so I asked a question. "Would this not be the province of religion and priests?"

"Codswallop, David. It requires the extended journey into the wilderness of the inner being to obtain enlightenment. Those who have done so find that the limitations of the dual nature of reality, and of language, make it impossible to communicate the spiritual truths they experienced, so they speak in paradoxes and riddles to reveal to others a sense of the revelations. Followers of enlightened ones who have not journeyed within themselves cannot comprehend fully, and so spiritual truths are tainted with secular ideas of ethics and mythologies, which ultimately develop into religious dogmas and rituals. Certainly, the role of the priests is to help their people, but the main function of the priestly class is to maintain and protect the dogma and the mythology of their religious order. Spirituality, by necessity, is an individual endeavor, but its benefits can and do radiate out for the welfare of the tribe. Seeking and searching for spiritual truths does not result always in enlightenment, but the very act of seeking is advantageous for the individual and by extension for the tribe."

"How do monks and monasteries fit in with this?" I wondered. "They meditate."

"Monks ostensibly seek spirituality and enlightenment for themselves by remaining secluded from the world within their enclaves. Monastic orders require strict adherence to specified rules and routines within the confines of the cloisters that separate them from the world. Monastic orders are usually attached to orthodox religions and monks are bound to accepted creeds — to conform to beliefs formalized by councils. This is usually legitimized by pronouncing that the councils speak for their deity. Although monks try to isolate themselves from temptations and human failings, by the monastic structure they are intricately bound to the same callous standards that have no real congruity with the dynamic flow of life rhythms. Most religious and monastic traditions rightfully admonish against the ravaging consequences of egoism and desires, but the relation to the rest of creation and to the power of the primordial forces is subordinated. Their isolation fosters a loss of proportion with an inability to comprehend the bigger picture. Spirituality requires embracing the world. Enlightenment is to be fully aware of the universe's workings, to become vitally alive in life's movement, the spiritual rhythm fusing with the movement of living things. The result is freedom and happiness."

The night breeze gently drifted in from the ocean, dissipating the mist around me, and the familiar salty dampness on my skin was comforting. The stars appeared bright and sparkling, and I could see the haze of the Milky Way. Li-Dan the fish ducked under the water, then resurfaced and swam to the water's edge. He propped upon his fish fins, and the moonlight shimmered off his glistening scales. I scooted closer, and we gazed intently at each other before continuing our conversation. It was remarkable the expressions he could make with a fish face.

I thought about what he said. "I've read stories about sages living in remote caves in mountains to meditate and find enlightenment. How is that different from the monks in cloisters?"

"Did I jargogle you?" Li-Dan fish-smiled, and I just shook my head at the silliness of it. "It is very different. Enlightenment is a slow process, David. Sages have experienced the world. They entwine in life's duality to enhance their understanding of the universe. They do not cut themselves off from life's movement in the world. Rather, they share their ever-increasing wisdom with those around them. With thought and meditation, they can help their tribe comprehend the creation more perfectly. As sages become totally harmonized to nature and the forces around them, their consciousness becomes radiant and powerful, and they are ready for the final transformation. Then, the sages retire to the seclusion of mountain caves and other isolated places to be undisturbed as they fully integrate the primordial forces with their bodies and minds, to vibrate at higher and higher frequencies as the transformations move to completion."

"Li-Dan, you said the Dragon Mother wanted you to tell me about dragons. What does all this have to do with dragons?"

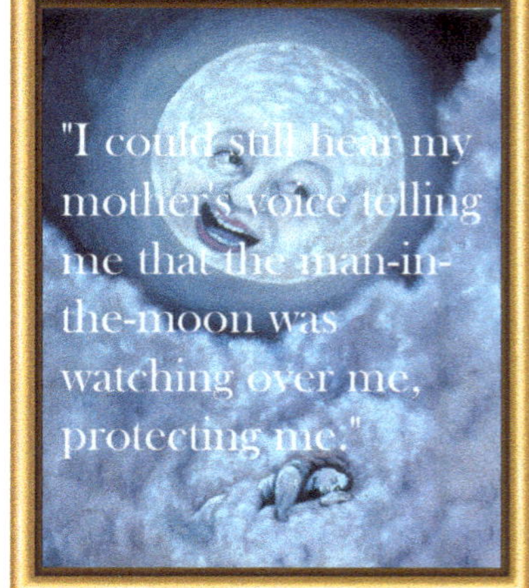

"David! Do you feel that I am bamboozling you? Do you fancy me a snollygoster?" Li-Dan asked with a dead-serious fish face.

"Li-Dan, I know you are having fun playing word games with me, but I really want to know about dragons. This is something important for me to understand."

"Indeed, it is. Okay, let's see, where to start?" He sat quietly for a few moments, and his ogling fish eyes drifted over to gaze upon the moon.

My gaze followed his, and looking upon the moon's silvery glow, I saw the same face in the moon that I did as a small child. I could still hear my mother's voice telling me that the man-in-the-moon was watching over me, protecting me. The feelings of security and gratitude I felt as a small boy came back. It was a magical moment those many years ago, and now once again, I sensed magic quivering all around me. Something wonderful was about to happen, and my life would change forever. I looked down, and Li-Dan was watching me with his absurd little fish smile.

Li-Dan the fish, also known as Lao Tzu, began: "It is always best to start at the beginning;

unfortunately, the beginning cannot be known. How can those from the duality comprehend in any way that which is not part of the duality? To answer what was at the beginning, we must say 'nothing,' for to us nothing can be understood outside of our existence. However, 'in the beginning' perhaps there was a singularity of consciousness, potentiality, and intention that we can ascribe to the Creator. From consciousness, potentiality, and intention came forth the primordial forces of creativity, magic, and love, which generated a spiritual force when they synchronized their rhythms. The spiritual force activated the primal energy force of the universal vibration, which brought into being duality. Within the duality, the spiritual force also shaped the primal elements of fire, water, earth, and air, which then led to the creation of the first life form — the dragons. The dragons, with their supernatural control of all the forces, forged the material world of the plants and animals, and finally the existence of humans."

"Did you understand all of that, David?" As I was watching Li-Dan the fish, it appeared that he had grown, and there were subtle changes in his appearance, but I put that aside and attempted to answer his question.

"I think so. In the unknowable singularity was consciousness, potentiality, and intention; which birthed the primordial forces of creativity, magic, and love that combined to form the primordial spiritual force; which led to the universal vibration and duality; which formed the primal elements of fire, water, earth, and air; which resulted in the creation of dragons, and led to the formation of the material world of plants, animals, and ultimately humans."

"Good," Li-Dan said. "And the primordial forces, individually and together as the spiritual force, continue to act and interact on the vibrational duality of the cosmos, and on the primal elements and all life in the material world. Not only that, but the primordial forces move through the entire cosmos with their own rhythms, rhythms that generate assorted patterns, such that the entire cosmos becomes as a living being.

"The primordial forces originated from non-duality. They do not have dual natures; thus, nor does the spiritual force. They are absolute; meaning they are pure, complete, free from imperfection — the conscious intention of the Creator. The primordial forces are ever-present within the cosmos of duality, their rhythms interacting with the forces of nature and all life.

"Herein lies the human dilemma. People live a shadowy existence — imperfect, incomplete, and transitory. Their rhythms of mind and body have the potential to interact and synchronize with the primordial rhythms, but their dual nature constantly intrudes. They are subjected to the principle of yin-yang, but finding the balance is always a struggle. Human love, creativity, and magic are not absolute, but rather are restrained by their opposites.

"David, imagine being able to access the pure power of the primordial rhythms by being in synchronization with them, and thus in harmony with the whole of creation. Creativity, to give shape and form to intention, imagination, and potential. Magic, to understand the dual principles of life, to bring the possible out of the impossible, and to have an influence over the forces of nature. Love, to emanate a profound, unrestrained affection for all of creation. And with all the forces synchronized into the spiritual force, to have a glimpse of the wonder of the Creator, of the infinite, freeing the human spirit. This is the goal of enlightenment, David."

Li-Dan stopped talking and looked deeply into my eyes to emphasize the gravitas of his words, but after a moment, he said playfully, "Now, it is time to talk about dragons." After the seriousness of his conversation so far, I was glad of the lighter tone.

"As I said, dragons are the first creatures of creation, given dominion over the four primal elementals — fire, water, earth, and air. The dragons are supernaturally created and are the origin of all creatures on the earth, and the dragons alone are divinely endowed with supernatural powers. With the dominion of the primal elementals, the dragons' domain is the seas and waters, clouds, winds, and rain; and their powers are the control of their life-giving and life-destroying natures. Dragons have the power of sending the gentle, nourishing rain or withholding it at their pleasure, of raising destructive tempests, or pacifying them. Dragons control all life forces with their supernatural power, but they are material beings of the earth. They are the living manifestation of the duality of the cosmos. Dragons fuse the spiritual and the material of heaven and earth.

"Dragons utilize the forces at work in the universe to control primal elementals, and in doing so, fire, water, earth, and air become living energies acting and reacting on each other. The dragons that I have talked about so far are one class of dragons, the earthly dragons. There are also celestial dragons and spiritual dragons, and although these two classes of dragons share the look and general nature of earthly dragons, they are of a different origin and have a different purpose. Later, I will tell you of the celestial dragons, but for the rest of the night let us discuss the earthly dragons."

I resettled myself upon the sand, assumed a relaxed pose, took a few deep breaths, and readied myself for an interesting night. Li-Dan, undeniably bigger with some features changed, but still a brilliantly shining, silver and red fish, started his story.

Portrait of a Red Dragon

6

The Earthly Dragons

Laurence Binyon

i-Dan talked as the moon finished its journey across the sky, the man-in-the-moon no longer discernable in his upside-down state. It was not a long night to me, for Li-Dan's rich, clinging-clanging voice kept me enthralled with his narrative about the earthly dragons. He no longer played his silly word game, but he seemed to genuinely enjoy the telling. I enjoyed the listening.

I think it best if I relate the dragon narrative myself, since so much information jumbled out over the course of the night. Long ago I shared that night with Li-Dan learning about dragons, but I remember it well, and over the years my understanding of dragons has grown. The first thing I will tell you is — dragons are real! Hard to believe? To the question as to why no one has seen a dragon in recent times, the answer is because it is not time for active doing. What that means will be apparent as the narrative unfolds. For now, understand that dragons are not in a current state of activity. A thousand years or so ago, they were, and there are still some isolated areas of the world where the local people are aware of their existence. When dragons are active, they are everywhere; in the heavens, on the land, and in the sea, influencing and directing the affairs of all life.

Even though earthly dragons are not divine, they do have a special place in creation as the first created, and the only creature with supernatural powers, but born, living, and dying on the earth. The life span of dragons is many thousands of years due to their supernatural nature, and also because they hibernate for great periods of time, conserving themselves. Hibernation comes when it is not time for active doing. During the winter they hibernate in caves or, more frequently, in deep waters, but on the spring equinox, they rise to the sky to establish their individual territories. Dragons are solitary creatures, each seeking out and defending its territory, but herds of dragons have been seen in the past. As the end of an Age of Humankind draws near, dragons do not rise at all, staying in hibernation to preserve the strength they will need.

The fundamental element in the dragons' power is the control of water, both the benevolent and the destructive aspects of water. In a sense, dragons are the personification of water. Water and wind are formless, transitory, and ever-changing, attuned to the dragons' nature. Dragons' domain is fire, water, earth, and air, so their power influences wind, lightning, rain, and the caverns of inaccessible mountains. The expelled breath of a dragon can form rain clouds, and thus the fertilizing rain that nourishes the crops is the dragon's breath of life.

Dragons are usually mild creatures. They expect the proper respect and veneration that by their wisdom and powers they are due, and when treated with respect, they are most benevolent and helpful. Undoubtedly, there are times when dragons have poor judgment in using lightning or flooding rains carelessly; yet, in general, they are kind in answer to the proper requests for rain when the crops need it. The dragons' mood can change abruptly when sufficiently provoked, or when fighting for or defending territory. Then dragons become fierce and rough creatures capable of terrible destruction. As they wind their way into the sky with the frenzy of hurricane winds, lightning, and inundations, the people and the land below are devastated.

The response is particularly severe when dragons are subjected to active mistreatment. Europeans have always slandered and abused dragons, making the hunting and killing of them the finest deed for a hero. Dragons, being proud and noble creatures, were not submissive to this treatment. They hoarded earth's treasures, ravaged the countryside at will, and did not bother to give their blessing to such insolent people.

Although dragons' escaped breath forms clouds, they also avail themselves of the clouds to cover their bodies, becoming invisible. It is said that dragons disappear as the clouds dissipate. They live in pools of water and rise into the air when the wind rises. They translocate into the air without any mechanical means. They do not have wings; rather, they use their supernatural control of the primal elementals to move about. Their supernatural nature also gives them the ability of transformation. Their forms can shift and change at will, sometimes as a silk worm or so large the limits of their bodies cannot be seen. Dragons often transform into other animals, particularly fish, if they wish to hide their true nature. When they desire to have direct contact with human life, they will usually assume the shape of an old man or a beautiful woman.

Dragons' breath can make water, but it can make fire, too. Dragons' fire and human fire are opposites. If dragons' fire encounters wetness, it flames, and if it meets water, it burns. Human fire can stop dragons' fire from burning and can extinguish the flames. Dragons are fond of flying by night and vomiting fire across the sky. It is a brilliant light show, rippling in a rhythm across the night sky in all directions, usually without their attending thunderous roars.

The dragons' vital spirit lies in the eyes. The dragons manifest their supernatural power through their eyes, and their eyes are terrible to behold. It is best to avoid looking directly into dragons' eyes, because there is so much power that it is dazzling, if not dangerous, to humans. Their eyesight is so powerful that dragons can see a mustard plant from a hundred miles, and at night a brilliant light shines from the glittering eyes.

When something of a miraculous nature occurs, those who live it know the truth of it. As time passes, the miracle becomes legend. As more time passes, and subsequent generations cannot envision the truth of it, it becomes myth. Finally, the miracle is totally dismissed and moves into the realm of fantasy. And thus it is with dragons. Chinese civilization, from the most ancient incarnation to the present, has had the greatest connection with dragons, and the greatest respect for them. Dragons taught the Chinese the making and use of the ideographic characters by which their language is written, as well as their understanding of the principle of yin-yang, and trigrams, a system of divination. The Chinese description and knowledge of dragons are indisputable.

The ancient Chinese view of the material world tends to put importance on the function of something, its relationship with other things, what it does, and where it is found. The Chinese have closely observed and understood dragons; consequently, their classification system has validity. All dragons belong to the genus lung. Within the genus lung, there are five kinds of earthly dragons, with the distinction based upon their color — white, black, red, azure, and yellow. All of these species of dragons are alike, but with some minor differences in temperament. The dragon found in the sky is given the species name lung, so the genus-species name is Lung-lung. When the dragon is in the sea, the species is li, and the genus-species name is Li-lung. The dragon found in the marshes is Kiau-lung, and the dragon of the earth that marks out the courses of rivers and streams is Ti-lung.

The dragons' whole existence is the essence of yin-yang. From their mouths, they can produce either water (yin) or fire (yang). They are of the earth (yin) but possess supernatural powers from heaven (yang). Their dominion is the water (yin), but they are powerful, forceful creatures of the sky (yang). Much of their life is spent quietly hibernating and waiting (yin), yet when the dragons are called into activity, they are vigorous and fierce in their fury (yang).

To humankind, dragons represent both light and darkness. Life, fertility, food, comfort, and beauty come from the clouds and rain. The sweet water that drops from the skies and flows from the mountains is for the happiness of humankind; but violent, destructive rain with wind, floods, and lightning is also dragon rain, a curse for all humanity. Dragons are the living symbol of the duality of all human morality; the eternal contrast and struggle between the constructive and destructive tendencies within everyone.

As dragons moved into myth and fantasy, they became the victims of grave injustices. With a singular lack of respect for the integrity of these noble creatures, fantasy writers and illustrators consistently misrepresented dragons by depicting them in all kinds of fantastic shapes and forms. The numerous attempts to relate dragons to extinct monsters and prehistoric lizards were made by people devoid of any knowledge of the distinctive features of dragons and their history.

The serpentine shape of the dragon is divided into three segments; from head to shoulder, from shoulder to breast, and from breast to tail. Large scales like those of a carp cover the body except for the belly. The belly is soft like a clam. On the dragon's throat, the large scales lie in reverse direction. This is a very sensitive area to the dragon, and to touch these scales is death to the offender. The scales of the male dragon number eighty-one. The female dragon has fewer.

Down the back is a line of bristling dorsal spines that run around the tip of the tail. Flame-like appendages emanate from the hips and shoulders. Those on the shoulders have the appearance of small wings. The two pairs of legs are shaped like those of a monitor lizard. The paws are like the paws of a tiger and are armed with the talons of a bird of prey. All dragons have four claws, except the yellow dragons, which have five.

The dragon's head is shaped generally like that of a scowling camel, except that the nostrils are flared farther apart. On top of the head is a big lump, called alternately the poh shan or the chih muh. This resembles a large pearl of bluish color, and it is striated with symbolic lines.

Without this important lump, the dragon is unable to ascend to the sky, but it is not clear why. I speculate it has something to do with resonance with the primordial rhythms, activating the supernatural power. Located to the sides and just behind the poh shan is a set of horns. These stag-like horns are straight or slightly undulating, of moderate length, and often have one or two small protuberances at the base. The eyes are like that of a hare with a kind of demonical stare to them that is quite frightening to behold. The ears are large like a bull's.

The mouth has the ferocity of a tiger's mouth, usually open with whiskers like the barbels of a catfish. The teeth are the sharp, pointed type carnivores need for tearing flesh; they add immensely to the dragon's demonic appearance. The long, slender tongue issues forth like a flame of fire. When dragons are peaceful, their voice is like the jingling of copper coins, but when dragons are in a fury, their voice thunders like the banging of large, copper pots. On the chin is a small, pointed beard, and under that a large pearl — the pearl of potentiality, almost half as big as the head of the dragon, embedded in an iguana-like neck. The pearl is white or bluish with a reddish or golden halo and a dark-colored, antler-shaped appendage rising from the center of the pearl's sphere. Both the pearl of potentiality and the poh shan are symbolic of the dual influences of nature and the forces, being portents, which if understood, benefit humankind. The symbolism

notifies humanity that all inhabitants of the world live under the sway of heaven and earth —
and nature, and to secure happiness, people must live in perfect harmony with those influences.

Dragons are male and female with some physical differences, although their basic natures
are the same. They tend to be the same size, which can be very large, but the male has horns,
deeper-set eyes in the sockets, and nostrils flared farther apart. He has a beard and compact
scales. The male body is strong toward the head and diminishing toward the tail. The male
dragon moves with a violent, writhing motion.

The female dragon has no horn, no beard, a straight nose, and eyes that bulge out of the head.
The muzzle or snout is straight-cut, the mane curly or rounded, and the scales sparse. Her body
is stronger at the tail, and she moves with a wavelike action. There is nothing vague or arbitrary
about the look of the dragons; like all other creatures on the planet, their appearance is specific
and unique. As with humans, there are distinctive features and differences of demeanor in each
individual dragon.

Since earthly dragons are of different sexes, naturally they reproduce their kind. Dragons
locate the opposite sex through their marvelous sight, whereupon they enter a combative type
of courtship behavior. This courtship is basically a dragon fight that is akin to their duels of
rivalry and territory. These courtship duels often place the countryside in danger, for they
are accompanied by tornadoes, thunderstorms, and devastating rains. The courtship fighting
helps instigate glandular actions involved in the mating process. The climax of this duel is
copulation, as the dragons wrap themselves in a belly-to-belly embrace. The period of union
is brief, but they copulate scores of times during the fight. This causes another problem for the
hapless people below, for often sperm rains down upon them, destroying crops and fouling the
water. When this occurred in the past, people burned a mixture of bones and filth to make a
foul smudge to drive away the mating dragons. Sometimes that worked; other times it did not.

Conception does not always occur, but when it does, the male dragon calls out, making a
breeze from above, and the female calls, making a breeze from below. The female usually has
only one egg, since the survival of the species does not depend on the production of many young.
Because of the dragons' supernatural nature, they live long lifetimes with low mortality rates.

Dragon eggs are shaped like the eggs of a hen, but they are much larger. They do not weigh
very much and give off a hollow sound when thumped. Quite often the shell is striated with

as many as five different colors. The eggs resemble the beautiful stones that can be picked up in the mountains or at a riverside. What makes these eggs so unique is their peculiarity of constantly producing water that seeps out through the shell.

The fetuses live in the eggs for a long time. Quite often, someone picks up an egg to admire the colors and shape and is fascinated by the water seepage. This is always dangerous, for woe unto the unfortunate person who possesses the egg at the time for hatching. When the egg is about to hatch, the dragon fetus inside makes a sound. The sound of the male dragon fetus makes the wind rise; whereas, the sound of the female fetus causes the wind to abate and change its direction. Then the egg cracks open and a dragon shaped like a small worm or snake creeps out. In a few moments, it begins to grow larger and larger amid a violent thunderstorm, dark and ominous, until the dragon, fully formed and with a terrible noise, forces its way up into the sky, smashing everything is its path.

As I mentioned before, dragons have the teeth of carnivores, and even though they will eat almost any kind of animal, their preference is for the larger mammals. Cattle, horses, and other domestic animals make the easiest game for them. In many areas of the world in the past, people learned the wisdom of giving cows or other livestock as sacrifices to their local dragon. Not only did this encourage the dragon to produce the necessary rain, but it kept the herds from being decimated. The prey is either ripped into pieces and devoured or, with the dragon assuming a vast size, swallowed whole. Dragons eat less than one might suppose. They hibernate much of the time, conserving themselves, but also their supernatural connection with the primordial forces keeps their bodies nourished and energized. Although food is nature's way for a living being to obtain energy, part of the dragons' essence is a self-generating energy source.

Fish are never eaten, for they are within the dragons' domain and are very special to them. Dragons have nothing to do with tigers. I know this sounds strange, but there is something about the nature of tigers that is antithesis to dragons. Not only will they not eat tigers, but dragons generally avoid tigers altogether. Dragons are known to attack elephants, not so much to eat the flesh, but they covet the elephant's blood, and they can subdue and drain an elephant rather rapidly. Curiously, the dragons' favorite treats are swallows. They are so ravenous for the swallow's flesh that it is advisable for anyone who has eaten of swallows to avoid crossing or coming near water, lest the dragon whose home is in the deep should devour the person to secure the dainty morsel inside.

This brings us to a sensitive matter, concerning earthly dragons killing and eating humans. Dragons do not need to consume that much food, so there is no need to kill or eat humans, and they will not do so unless they are abused or attacked first. Dragons are neither good nor evil, for they exist on a special level of existence, balanced between the primordial forces and the rhythms of the material world. Dragons are noble creatures, superior in every way to humans. Typically, they assist humankind. People in a village or town near a body of water that is the abode of a dragon should give that dragon the proper respect for its wisdom, dignity, and superiority, as well as for the dragon's control over the rainfall. Paying formal respect is important because if the dragon is not kept in good humor, the crops might be endangered by insufficient rainfall. The dragon protects and benefits the people of its territory. When the dragon is abused, it responds in like manner. The dragon never strikes without provocation.

Humans, because of their erect stature and sentient nature, see themselves as the princes of creation, godlike even, for they invariably cast their assorted deities in the image of themselves. This leads to the desire to extend their dominion over the dragons, which is what happened in Europe and the British Isles, so that killing dragons became heroes' noble deeds. Most incidents of people being killed and eaten by dragons come from there, where dragons were despised, maligned, and treated as demons.

Dragons are extremely difficult to defeat. Unless completely cut, dragons can rejoin severed skin. They also sometimes shed their scales, which shine in the darkness. Dragons are repelled by iron. They cannot tolerate it in their water and will flee from it in a rage. It has something to do with the pungent nature of iron, perhaps, distressing their eyes, which are where their vital spirit lies. As a result, those attempting to kill a dragon knew to use iron weapons in their attacks. Dragons are reputed to abhor centipedes. I don't know why, but I am repulsed by them, too. I cannot imagine that "heroes" used centipedes to assault dragons, but it is possible, I suppose. They would certainly need every advantage to defeat a dragon.

Another incentive for people attacking dragons is their purview of the earth elemental. Dragons are known to have caches of precious stones, gems, gold, and minerals, which they store in deep mountain caves or in the seas' depths.

There are other treasures that would incite a person to attempt an attack on a dragon. Dragon saliva is a lovely, purple hue and, in the past, was highly treasured by rulers and the wealthy for making the most exquisite of perfumes. Dragon spittle has an extremely powerful odor, disagreeable in its concentrated form, but very effective when diluted and blended with other odors. The spittle not only adds a pleasant quality to perfumes but possesses a long-lasting attribute that can fix or prolong the life of some other odor mixed with it. It can bind camphor and musk for several tens of years without evaporating. When the spittle mixture is burned as incense, a fragrant, blue smoke wafts through the air.

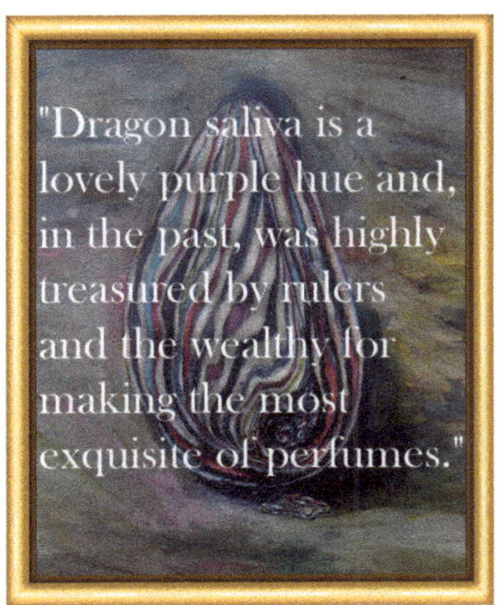

The saliva is most commonly gathered from the sea surface or when it washes ashore. Hardened by the sun, the saliva forms a waxy substance, grayish or amber-colored, that floats in hard pieces on the water. It has been found floating or washed upon the beach in masses as large as two hundred pounds, but it is still very expensive.

Another source of saliva is the froth produced by fighting dragons, which rains down upon the earth in copious amounts. It is difficult to collect since it is scattered and diluted so much by the wind and rain. An effective method of gathering spittle is to give the dragon a swallow in a slow and deliberate fashion. This makes the dragon's mouth water with a large quantity of saliva dripping down that is easy to collect — easy, if the dragon is not annoyed that you did not bring two swallows.

The blood of some dragons is red, of others, black. When a dragon's blood enters the earth, it becomes amber-colored. Dragon's blood has value to humans because drinking the blood confers knowledge of the bird's language. Eating a dragon's heart enables one to acquire the knowledge stored in this "organ of the mind," so that not only the bird's language but all creatures' language is understood. Obviously, this does not mean that one talks in bird-speak. It refers to the ability to comprehend what the bird or other animal is communicating to others of its species.

The fat from a dragon is particularly useful. Silk garments soaked in it are impermeable to water. When lit, the fat spreads such a brilliant light that it can be seen for a hundred miles. This is what Li-Dan told me but, honestly, to obtain the spittle, blood, and fat of dragons is almost certainly a lethal undertaking, and I question the risk to the potential reward.

Dragons lose some of their scales and teeth often in their aerial battles, and once in a thousand years, dragons slough off skin and scales. Being mortal, earthly dragons can and do die and decay. People in ancient times found dragons' bones, teeth, horns, and scales and became well-versed in their curative powers. On mountains and cavernous cliffs, on all places where dragons raise clouds and rain, dragon detritus can be found, especially scales and teeth. The bones and horns are usually buried deeply in the earth, or in the seas' depths.

The curative power of dragons' parts is attributed to the strong yang virtue in them, which effectively drives the yin demons out of the body. This was the thought in ancient times, but the dragons' remnants are still infused with the primordial forces' influences as essence of the dragons' being, and this is powerful. The best bones are those having five colors, which, corresponding to the five visceral parts of the human body — the liver, lungs, heart, kidneys, and spleen — significantly aids in their healing. The fresh, hard bones are not the ones to use, but rather bones that are old and brittle. Thin, broad-veined bones are from female dragons; those coarse with narrow veins are from the males.

There are various methods for preparing the dragons' bones for medicinal use; for example, soaking them in spirits for a night, then drying and rubbing them to a powder. Some bones are poisonous and need to be prepared with great care. Iron instruments and utensils should be avoided. When a physician uses the bones, knowledge of the dragons' nature, their likings, and their hatreds is necessary to properly prepare them. Dragon medicine heals a long list of ailments, but the reason for the medicines' effectiveness is the residual potency from the dragon's vital spirit.

This was what Li-Dan told me about the earthly dragons that moonlit night. While listening through the night, I was dazed as the reality of dragons washed over me. I did not interrupt Li-Dan with questions; instead, I let his telling soak deeply into me. When I refocused my eyes, Li-Dan the fish at the ebb tide's edge had become Li-Dan the not-quite-a-fish. Looking gently at me, he said to meet him there at the turtle dune on the ninth full moon. I nodded. Then, misty clouds poured out of his mouth, covering his body. I glimpsed reddish, glowing shapes within, twisting and turning. The clouds dissipated as quickly as they had formed, and there, standing in the retreating surf, was a majestic, red dragon, a dragon exactly as Li-Dan had described.

I whispered, "Li-Dan, you take my breath away. You are an earthly dragon!"

"No, David. I am something else." Then Li-Dan the red dragon churned round and round, the surf spinning. Throwing his head back, he roared like gonging thunder, and, with a powerful updraft of wind, he spiraled into the rose-colored clouds of morning, and he was gone!

I sat there for a few minutes, watching the clouds tint to orange as the sun peeked over the horizon. Weariness settled into me, and I decided to forgo my morning meditation session. I trudged dully home, did not take off my sandals at the door, thumped up the stairs, and found my bed. I flopped down, fully clothed and smelling of the salted air, and fell asleep immediately.

Wise Men on a Dragon

7

The Story of Tung Fu

*"One who lives in accordance with nature
does not go against the way of things.
He moves in harmony with the present moment
always knowing the truth of just what to do."*

Tao Te Ching, Verse 8 by Lao Tzu

hen I awakened hours later, the sun was high in the sky, and I was slightly disoriented. Disrupted sleep pattern, I figured. Stumbling downstairs, I made my way into the kitchen for coffee. Sand was scattered on the floor of the house, marking my early morning path to the bedroom. I smiled and thought, that's how it should be; sand as nature's talisman from the beach, an ever-present reminder of the sacredness of living by the ocean.

With a mug of coffee in hand, I made my way, barefooted and shirtless, to the bench at the beach access. Settling myself with legs crossed, I stared out over the breaking surf and thought about dragons. How could I not?

The image of Li-Dan, the red dragon, was burned into my inner sight. Over and over, I reviewed every detail of his magnificence, until finally I decided to draw Li-Dan's dragon portrait. The portrait was begun that afternoon, and it was the first of a series of dragon drawings that I made over the next nine months. I kept all the drawings playful and fun. I am not sure why I did that; it just seemed right. On rag paper, I smeared, brushed, dabbed, and wiped washes of paint, creating rhythm and movement to stimulate my imagination to see the image I wanted to illustrate. Using a No. 2 yellow pencil, I drew what my mind's eye saw in the wash. With different colors of very thin paint, all the shapes were blocked in to set the overall field and color relationships. Then the entire image was executed with a complex buildup in the rich, lush colors of wax crayons. The final stage turned on the lights using touches of opaque paint. Creating those drawings was so much fun that I added a series of illustrations about the Dragon Mother's story of Hana's Promise.

Each month on the full moon, my evening meditation was in my bedroom, just in case the Dragon Mother came to me. On the sixth month of full moons, she finally did. I was in my usual seated position on the bed, deep into a peaceful, relaxing state of mind, when the soft, jingling-jangling voice of the Dragon Mother inserted itself gently into the serenity. "Come to the In-Between. You have been here, so you can find your way. Focus your vision of the In-Between in a calm, relaxed manner. Do not struggle; acquiesce to the way here. Allow it to happen. I am waiting for you."

Believe it or not, I did it. It took a little while, but as I continued to meditate, I began to grasp her instructions. Instead of going within to the rhythms of my mind and body, I used my meditation to go within the In-Between, reaching out to its rhythm, wrapping my mind around it, and gently synchronizing myself to become one with it.

"Hello, David. It is lovely to see you again," the Dragon Mother jingled as she emerged from the bluish mist, smiling and radiant. She was in her human form, not as a dragon, her satiny gown flowing around her tucked-under legs, sitting by a babbling brook. Yes, I said a "babbling brook." I know it's trite, but truly, the brook was babbling a whispery, enchanting song as it cascaded over the smooth stones, striped with many colors.

It was a genuine joy to see the Dragon Mother again. She had on a different gown from the last time I saw her. Elegant, with shiny gold embroidery of vines and leaves, the gown was as majestic as she was. Subtly pulsing as if alive, a pearl on a golden chain graced her neck. Ebony hair, sparkling with highlights of blue, curled its way down her back. Her eternal beauty was heightened by her ageless wisdom.

"Dragon Mother, I am happy to be with you again," I beamed.

"And I, you. Did you enjoy your time with Li-Dan?" asked the Dragon Mother as she arose and slowly walked along the stream bank. She moved effortlessly, fluidly, as if her bare feet glided; every movement was gracefully in harmony and committed to that one act of walking. I hobbled along beside her.

"Very much, but talking with a fish about dragons was weird. I kept wondering if I was dreaming or in some sort of trance."

The Dragon Mother nodded her understanding. "Minds become ingrained with habitual and acceptable methods of thinking. It is often difficult to clear the mind of prejudiced ways of comprehending reality. What is tragic about that is the way one's mind chooses to interpret the world affects and changes one's reality in the world — advantageously or not. The magical rhythm is ever present. The impossible becomes possible, the nothing becomes something, the fantastic becomes real; magic latches onto the transitory, impermanent, indistinct, imperfect, and incomplete. For you, my suggestion is to accept the purity of what you saw, heard, and felt. Trust your senses, for sometimes it is necessary to let go of a biased mindset to truly discern what is presented to you."

In a conciliatory tone, I said, "I suppose that I already have, for I have begun colorful drawings of the dragons of which Li-Dan spoke."

"I know, and I am delighted," she laughed.

"How do you know? Can you watch me from the In-Between?" The ramifications of that disturbed me.

She could see consternation flickering across my eyes. The Dragon Mother reassured me, "No, David, I cannot watch you, but when you are in deep-state meditation, the primordial rhythms of the universe synchronize more forcefully with your mind, and you touch the In-Between, allowing me to sense and access your rhythms. Your creative rhythm is so energetic that it's difficult for me not to tap into it. People who are rich in their connections to the forces of creativity, magic, or love always are at the edge of the In-Between. When all three together as the spiritual rhythm are abundant within someone, this is especially true. It has always been so."

As we walked, following the water's flow, I thought about love. "Dragon Mother, you mentioned love; I have been in love and lost that love. It was very painful."

With a small, wistful smile, she said, "I know that pain, David." After a moment, she continued. "Love is a force generating a rhythm that circulates through the universe, revealing itself in a myriad of ways. The primordial rhythm of love, when embedded within the rhythms of your mind and body, affects all aspects of your life, including romantic love. The love rhythm is primal love; the various manifestations are expressions of that primal love. The antithesis of love is thought to be hate, but the impediments to being able to truly embrace love are ego, desire, and fear. If a manifestation of love goes awry, how does that in any way diminish the primal love? The pain, hurt, and anger from a love lost do not come from primal love; rather they are the actions of ego, desire, and fear. The control, or even elimination of these detriments, is within the purview of meditation. The more one meditates, David, the more a pure love is a part of one's life. You have come far in your meditations; perhaps you should be receptive to romantic love again." Perhaps so, I thought.

We reached a ledge where the water dropped into the mist below; the babbling brook roared on its way down. Dragon Mother sat down on the rocky ledge, dangling her feet over the precipice. She patted her hand on the ledge, inviting me to sit beside her. Heights have always been a problem for me, so I lowered myself gingerly beside her, but a little way back from the drop. Dragon Mother peered at me and smiled as she spoke. "I will tell you another wonderful story. It is the story of Tung Fu."

"The town of Zacát was perched at the edge of a plateau on an aged mountain range. The rounded mountains hugged a small river meandering deep in a ravine. Waterfalls spilled down to the river from the verdant slopes of the cloud forests. Pine trees covered the mountains: white pines, tall and stately; stunted yellow pines that tenaciously gripped craggy outcroppings; and smooth-barked pines with their elegant, long, floppy needles. Tucked in with the pines were gnarly, evergreen oaks and stands of firs, poking their pointy tops into the cloudy mists. Sheep and goat herds foraged around the whole town and among the pines, providing the means for the town to prosper.

"Zacát sprawled to the cliff, precariously hanging over, looking as if it would slide down the mountain at any time. The buildings were constructed of the abundant wood and stone and were centered around a church and a formal garden of carefully tended trees and shrubs. Beyond the town, the landscape undulated, with open fields interspersed with pine copses and thickets, forming a high valley as it rose almost imperceptibly to a dormant volcano, so green with pine forests that the townspeople were unaware of its existence. What should have given away its presence were odd basalt rock formations, born of ancient lava, and strewn all over the landscape. Each of the hundreds of rock formations stood solitary in tall, fantastic shapes, many given names based on their looks, but legend spoke dragons had formed each one. The area was known to the town of Zacát as the Dragon Valley.

"The town was cool and damp most of the year, with fog in the ravine below rising every day, often to bathe the town in a disorienting haze. On the top of the hidden volcano was a monastery built of basalt stone, jutting out from the pine forest like one of the unique rock formations in the Dragon Valley. A small stream crisscrossed the valley floor until it trickled over an enormous rock outcropping north of the town, descending to the river ravine below. There was a narrow switchback path down this outcropping leading to many shallow caves in the mountainside. However, no one in Zacát dared take this path, for in one of the caves lived a sage, said to have strange powers. He was seen only a few times a year. With long, unkempt dark hair and a beard partially obscuring his sharp, angular face, he looked like a wild man, so when he walked into town from time to time in his all-black, coarse clothing, the people of Zacát averted their eyes and gave him a wide berth. Had they bothered to look carefully, they would have noticed that under his dark, bushy eyebrows glittered blue eyes full of wisdom and peace. For as long as people could remember, he had lived in the caves. No one knew his name, but he came to be called 'Wildman.'

"The prosperous section of town was the center surrounding the church and park; the homes a mixture of stone and pine. The people of Zacát were for the most part decent and caring, just living their lives as best they could. They were devoted to the church and assisted others in the community. The town mayor was a good man, large of stature and girth, who earnestly cared for the Zacát people, and called everyone by name. He stroked his thick mustache when he pondered and had a booming voice and a hearty laugh. Everyone liked him and called him 'Mayor Memo.' The north area of town was less prosperous, the homes of wood, although well-kept. It was here that a widow by the name of Tung Mâh lived in a modest, two-room house.

"Tung Mâh's husband, Tung Fang, who fancied himself an adventurer, made a journey to the northern provinces to seek a purported mountain planted in fire, which neither the sun nor moon illuminated, but was lighted to its whole extent by the blue fire from a black dragon. He never returned. This happened when Mâh was a young woman and before they had a child. Mâh lived a quiet, peaceful life, working yarns of wool to support her simple needs. She always had a garden of vegetables and flowers, which she traded and shared with her neighbors. Of average height, she was slender with a dark complexion. Her joy was walking alone every evening among the stone structures in the Dragon Valley, as the evening breeze softly whistled through the towering stones. To Mâh, the stone formations were exotic sculptures created by unknown forces of nature, the visible expression of their presence.

"During these evening strolls among the stones, she often saw Wildman, as it was his habit to walk among them, too. Mâh would see him at times sitting quietly under a stone sculpture, legs crossed, hands on his lap, fingers posed in unusual positions, and eyes closed. She was not put off by his appearance, but rather, she was intrigued. They never spoke until one evening when Mâh was enjoying her evening walk with the full moon just over the distant mountain. In the moonlight, she spied Wildman sitting quietly under the stone statue that people called 'Dragon Rising.' Mâh sat down nearby at the stone statue known as 'Tiger Roaring' and mimicked Wildman's seated pose. With eyes closed, she sat there for quite a while, eventually becoming aware of subtle shifting wind, the moonlight filtered through the pines, and the beating of her heart softly swaying her body.

"Without opening her eyes, she sensed his close presence. A melodic voice with an odd chime to it said: 'Your pose is good; now control your breathing. Put your tongue to the roof of your mouth, and inhale slowly through your nose by smoothly expanding your belly; and then pause for a moment, before allowing the air to escape by effortlessly pulling it back in. Pause briefly again and repeat this over and over. The pause allows your mind and body to feel and move your energy, and it will help you to focus on the rhythms within you.'

"Mâh said nothing, kept her eyes closed, and attempted to follow Wildman's instructions. She became aware that he sat closely across from her, and she could hear his breathing. Soon, she was also aware that they were breathing in rhythm together, as one, and she felt her energy and his energy flowing back and forth between them with each breath. It was a delicate connection, but it was exhilarating.

"It was also intimate. Mâh had been alone since her husband died, and the affinity that she felt awakened deep sensations long dormant. Her whole body was vibrating at a more intense level. Everything around her — the stones, pines, plants, the wind moving, all — was richer and more intensely sensed. The comfortable, inner prison in which she had locked herself for years dissolved and she knew freedom. And happiness!

"In the evenings that followed, Mâh and Wildman met regularly under the stone sculptures and meditated together, always joining their breathing and rhythms into one. Then they would walk through the Dragon Valley, sometimes talking, sometimes in silence. They came to know and understand each other, and Mâh realized that the Zacát people were correct; Wildman had powers, powers that were related to understanding nature's workings, but he was also something more than a sage. What she did not know, nor did she care.

"The townspeople of Zacát were not judgmental; more importantly, they were not self-righteous. They fervently believed that everyone had the right to be happy and to choose the course of their own lives. The church itself fostered such a belief; the pastor saw herself as the humble shepherd of the people, helping them live full and rich lives. No controlling rites, dogmas, restrictions, or rules, except one: give only unconditional love and kindness to all. Of course, individuals varied in their ability to follow that one precept, but that belief was so imbedded in the town's spirit that adherence to it was the norm. Mâh was a very private person, and respecting privacy was important to the town as well, so her developing relationship with Wildman was not known to others. As she was close to the end of her child-bearing years, it was a great surprise to the town when she began to show her fecundity."

"I'm sorry. What?" I interrupted.

"She was pregnant, David."

"Oh."

Dragon Mother, amused, continued.

"The women of Zacát were helpful during Mâh's pregnancy, and several were present on the night she gave birth in the bedroom of her small house. They became uncomfortable when they noticed that the strange sage, Wildman, was sitting outside the front door under a bull pine tree. His legs were crossed in a meditational pose, his eyes closed, his body unmoving. As Mâh's labor became intense, she settled into a focused, breathing pattern to control her pain. Outside under the pine tree, Wildman was breathing the same focused pattern, perfectly in sync with Mâh, flowing their energies together as one, sharing the pain and the experience.

"When the head of the newborn crowned, the wind abruptly ceased blowing and a dead calm settled on the whole town. The women attending Mâh and everyone in the town stopped what they were doing and looked around, apprehensive, for they knew that something unusual was happening. As the baby boy was born and cried his first cry, a powerful gust of wind suddenly blasted in from the east. A thick, dark cloud bank rode that wind, rippling with lightning and rumbling with thunder; and as the townspeople stared up in awe, two azure dragons burst out of the massive clouds and with loud peals of gonging thunder flew down to the small house, landing on either side of the still meditating Wildman. The blue dragons turned their heads to look at the unmoving sage, as they regally strutted to positions of protection at the front door of Tung Mâh's house.

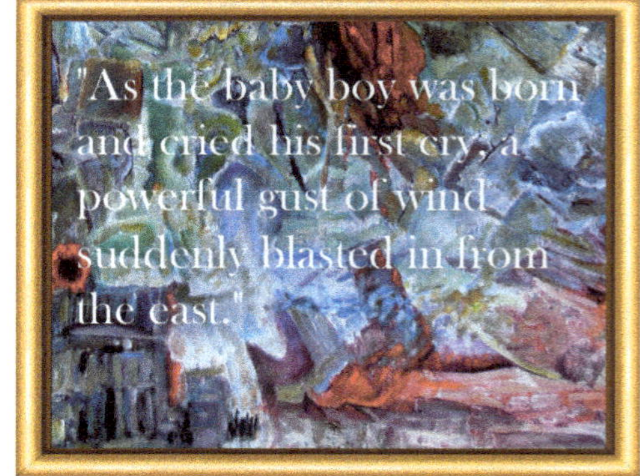

"The women attending Mâh trembled with fear, but they finished their assistance to the mother and child, then hastened out the door between the two dragons and ran to their homes. Mâh was weak from her labor, but she carried her newborn baby boy, snuggled at her breasts, to the front door, and after nodding respectfully to the azure dragons, who nodded back, she looked at Wildman, sitting under the pine tree, tenderly looking back at her. With a weary smile, she pronounced: 'His name is Tung Fu.' With that, Tung Mâh turned back to the bedroom to focus her love and attention on her newborn son. Wildman closed his eyes again to meditate. The azure dragons remained as guards at their posts. The sky cleared, and all was well in Zacát.

"Naturally, there was much discussion in town the next few days about the birth of Tung Fu and the appearance of two azure dragons. The consensus was that it was proper that two dragons appeared in their town, for the legends told that dragons had constructed the stone formations, the heart and soul of Zacát. And it was well-known that the sudden appearance of azure dragons was a good omen, portending nourishing spring rains and abundant crops. It also presaged that Tung Fu was destined for greatness, as he most assuredly was.

"The azure dragons were conspicuously present, walking authoritatively throughout the Dragon Valley and ever watching over Mâh and Fu. Mayor Memo and some of the citizens regularly offered sheep and goats to the dragons, in respect, and as a precaution to prevent their herds from wantonly being decimated. The dragons served as guardians over the Tung household for nine full moons. On the night of the ninth full moon, a powerful wind from the east blew into the Dragon Valley, then rose straight up into the clouds. Both azure dragons rode the wind up into the moonlit clouds, whereupon the clouds dissipated, along with the dragons.

"Many townspeople had run to the Dragon Valley to see what had happened. The dragons were gone, but there were two new, massive stone sculptures standing side by side in the moon's luminescence, facing toward Mâh's home and the town beyond. The sculptures became known in Zacát as the Protectors, a benevolent bequest from the azure dragons to Mâh and the town, acknowledging to all they were under the dragons' protection.

"Mayor Memo inquired of Abbot Basil of the monastery for any knowledge that he had about dragons. Abbot Basil was a learned man, knowledgeable in matters of the natural and arcane, and skilled in healing. The monastery was ancient, built long before the town of Zacát. Its archives were extensive, reaching back into the mystical past. The order was immersed in the contemplation of the spiral as revealed in nature. Their belief was that by understanding the spiral to its concentrated endpoint, it would allow them to experience the touch of the Creator. To this end, there was a well-known story of Abbot Basil, as a novice, who burnt a hole in the thatch of his dwelling to admire a spiral-shaped gloriole effect of moonlight; and in his rapture he failed to notice that he had set afire a whole section of the monastery. With his zeal, he was destined to become abbot.

"In their discussion, Abbot Basil related to the mayor that there was an ancient reference to an azure dragon who lived in the valley before the monastery was built. It was said that it was he who constructed the fantastic stone formations all through the valley. An itinerant group of monks walked into the valley one day, and from their prolonged wandering, they were weary and weak, both physically and spiritually. The monks took refuge in caves on the volcano mountaintop overlooking the valley. The dragon, who gave his name to the monks as Dàmo Lung, took pity on them, and began to teach and help them. Dàmo Lung opened their minds to the workings of nature and taught the monks how to be in harmony with the forces and rhythms around them, to heal them spiritually and physically. Further, Abbot Basil said, the reference speaks of the dragon Dàmo as assisting in building the monastery.

"Over the centuries, the lush beauty of the high valley and surrounding mountains attracted more people. The monastery increased its size and influence, and the town of Zacát was founded. Dàmo Lung taught the monks, who passed on those teachings to the Zacát people, so that they benefited from the wisdom of the azure dragon, and flourished. The community became a place of peace and serenity — the people, free and happy.

"The curious thing, said the abbot, was that one day there was a terrific storm — torrential downpour, furious winds, and lightning. When the storm was over, the azure dragon, Dàmo Lung, was gone, never to be seen again. It was also the first time the stranger with long, wild hair and beard, and dressed in black, was seen in the valley — the man who came to be known as Wildman.

"Wildman continued to live in his cliff cave, and Mâh and Fu in the small house. In the evenings, he walked and meditated in the valley. Mâh lovingly tended to her son, and after nine months of full moons, she began to take Fu with her to join Wildman in the valley. Many people of Zacát paid their respects to Mâh and her son, helping with chores around the house and in the garden. Mayor Memo was especially attentive, making sure their needs were met. He knew the event of Fu's birth portended something of great significance.

"The first few years of Fu's life passed quickly. Fu became an inquisitive little boy who enjoyed roaming freely in the Dragon Valley. Wildman spent much time with Fu, teaching him the nature of the four elementals, how they interacted and maintained balance together. Fu learned to feel the movement of life by sensing the omnipresent spiritual rhythm expressed upon the elementals of fire, water, earth, and air. He had an inborn grasp of all life's dynamic flow. By the time he was five, he had mastered deep meditation. His rhythms of creativity and magic were forceful, and he easily synchronized them with the primordial forces. Fu was precocious in drawing with the brush, with the ability to activate the rhythms of creativity and magic into his brushstrokes, as if breathing actual life into his drawings. By the time Fu was nine, he had mastered Wildman's teaching of the power of the vital spirit in the eyes. In his eyes the rhythms of his life projected and interacted with the world. Wildman taught Fu the technique, moving his energy to synchronize with or adversely affect the various rhythms around him. Wildman was pleased; so was Mâh.

"Abbot Basil called on Mâh one afternoon to invite Fu to visit the monastery. Mâh agreed that Fu could walk up the slope to the monastery the next morning. Fu left early the next day, ambling as a boy is wont to do among the stones and pines of the Dragon Valley. As he crossed the stream that meandered through the grassy valley, his eyes spied a large, smooth stone in the streambed. It was unusual, for the stone was striped with many colors, so in his curiosity, he plucked it out of the water. Fu turned the stone over to examine it. It was strangely light for its size, and the colors were varied, but natural in their tones, not overtly brilliant.

Fu could discern an unusual rhythm emanating from the stone. He knew that everything in nature has its own rhythm — Wildman taught him that. Things are not just things. Things — the material world — have forces within them, forming their essence. They connect intimately with other things, and with the ubiquitous external forces. Forces create rhythms, distinctive rhythms, which can be detected and acted upon. This Fu knew, and so, turning the stone over and over, he was sure this was not a stone, but what it was, he did not know. He put it in his satchel and journeyed on to the monastery.

"Abbot Basil greeted Fu at the wide gate and escorted him into the monastery courtyard. Several monks were busy sweeping up the pine needles and oak leaves. Older monks were carefully raking whitish soil in the center of the courtyard into undulating wavy patterns that spiraled in and around meticulously placed stones, connecting the stones into a unity of quiet, exquisite beauty, conducive to meditation and spiritual awareness. In one of the larger stones was a smoothly carved-out, round basin that held water and one small fish of orange and white. Fu could feel the rhythms of harmony and peace.

"Abbot Basil led Fu along a cloister spaced with stone containers of carefully tended, small, gnarled pine trees, and into the library. The library was lined and stacked with a myriad of books and scrolls. In the center was an oak table and chairs, darkened with age. The only window was covered with a paper shutter, the morning sunlight casting a perfect shadow of a pine branch upon it. Fu was transfixed by the purity of the image and stared at it for a long moment. Abbot Basil, watching Fu, nodded his head in approval.

"Fu sat down in an oak chair across from Abbot Basil, the chair diminishing his already small frame. Abbot Basil sat still for a moment, peering at the image on the window shutter. Then he shifted his eyes to the waiting eyes of Fu and said: 'It is essential to sweep the mind clear to perceive the truth and beauty of nature as it really is. This is the reason we in the monastery put so much attention to sweeping and raking, for in these repetitious activities, we can empty our minds. Do you understand?'

" 'Yes, Abbot. I have learned this from Wildman.'

"Abbot Basil responded curiously, 'Really? The Wildman?'

"Fu nodded his head and waited for the abbot to regain his focus. 'I asked you here, Fu, to see if you might be interested in taking the monastic vows and joining our monastery. It is a life of ascetic devotion and contemplation. The library here would be available to you to study and learn. Uh, do you know how to read, my son?'

"Fu nodded again and said, 'My mother taught me.'

" 'Yes, yes. Of course, she did. Well, what do you think, Fu? Would this interest you?'

"It was then that Abbot Basil became acutely aware of Fu's eyes, which were looking into his. They almost glowed, he thought, but what had his attention was the sudden sense of kindness and serenity that flowed over him ... from, from ... Fu. How is this possible, he thought?

" 'Thank you, Abbot Basil.' Fu's voice was soft and gentle. 'I would like to study the books in the library, but I belong in the Dragon Valley, among the trees and stones, and with the people of Zacát. Wildman is my teacher, and he is guiding me in understanding the world. I have much to learn from him, sir, but again, I thank you for your offer.'

"After a poignant moment of silence, the abbot sighed and slowly shook his head. 'I knew of the presence of your teacher in the valley, and the various rumors about him, but I never thought to engage him, to speak with him. It appears that I made a grave mistake.' Abbot Basil's eyes were lost in deep thought for a time, and then he looked upon the boy. 'Fu, you may visit the library at any time. I have spent most of my life in this room, reading and studying, and I will help you in any way that I can.'

"Fu remembered the stone he had found. Reaching into the satchel hung around his shoulder, Fu pulled out the striped stone and presented it to Abbot Basil. 'Sir, could you tell me what this is? It looks like a stone, but I can sense that it is not.'

"Abbot Basil took the stone from Fu and noticed that water was beading on its surface. Very curious, he thought, and at that moment, he heard a faint jingling-jangling sound and felt a stirring of the air in the room. A memory of something he had read years ago suddenly burst into his mind — and his eyes went wide and his face paled. He shoved the stone into Fu's hands.

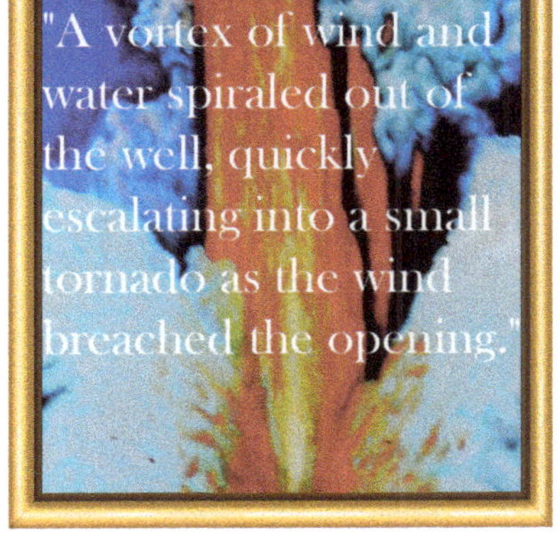

" 'Fu! Quickly, quickly, we must find water!' he screamed. 'The well! Run as fast as you can to the well and drop the stone into it! The well is out the door and down the corridor to the courtyard on the right.'

"Fu bolted as fast as he could down the cloister to the well and threw the stone into it. The stone clacked as it bounced off the walls, until it splashed into the water. The breeze across the monastery abruptly stopped, and dead silence hung in the stilled air for a few seconds. Fu instinctively backed away from the well. A gusting wind suddenly swept across the courtyard from the east carrying black clouds that darkened the sky. A roaring sound echoed up from the well. Now, Fu was in a dead run to the opposite side of the monastery with Abbot Basil shuffling as fast as he could behind him.

"Fu's ears pounded with a thundering swoosh as he stopped and looked back at the well. Abbot Basil and many monks were gawking at the well, too. A vortex of wind and water spiraled out of the well, quickly escalating into a small tornado as the wind breached the opening. Everyone inhaled a collective gasp as an azure dragon churned out of the tornado, vomiting lightning and rain out of its short muzzle, as it spiraled up into the clouds and disappeared.

"The destruction to the monastery was considerable, a whole section destroyed along with many pine trees, but the monks were oblivious to that. They were ecstatic to witness the rising of a female blue dragon amid a sacred spiral.

"Fu looked up to the beaming face of Abbot Basil. 'Sir, I am so sorry about the damage to your building. I didn't know what that stone was.'

" 'Oh, no, Fu. We can rebuild, but that was a miraculous phenomenon, an occurrence mentioned only in the most ancient of texts, and we were blessed to witness it. Thank you for bringing us the dragon's egg.'

"Fu hurried down the slope to the Dragon Valley, where he saw Wildman standing in front of the stone statue of 'Dragon Rising.' Fu started to tell his teacher about the azure dragon, but he stopped when he realized that Wildman already knew. In fact, as he looked around, he saw that many townspeople were still staring up at the monastery. Obviously, the catastrophic, yet wondrous event of the azure dragon rising was witnessed by the whole town. Wildman leaned over to Fu and whispered, 'It was Ti-Lung. I will help the monks rebuild the monastery.'

"Over the next few weeks, the lessons from Wildman began to include knowledge about dragons. Fu learned about their nature, their likes and dislikes, and the dragons' unique place in creation. Wildman gave to Fu a small cup of a thick and sticky liquid, deep red in color, almost black. Fu gave Wildman a reluctant look, but after bringing the cup to his nose and sniffing, he swallowed it in one gulp. Almost immediately, his senses became more vigorous. There was a clarity in the air he had never experienced. In the pine trees, birds were chirping, whistling, and singing. Fu understood them, not as words, but in the birds' intentions. All of Fu's senses were heightened and he was exhilarated by it.

"Wildman helped Fu to develop and control his internal energy, with the ability to project it into other living things. One day, Fu walked into the town on an errand for his mother, when he saw a small plant in a pot outside the woolen shop. The plant was unhealthy, scraggly with browning leaves. Fu crouched down by the potted plant and held his hands out over it. A small smile was on Fu's face as he softly hummed and gently sent his energy out through his palms. As his hands hovered, the leaves began to respond, moving when Fu's hands moved, growing and changing into a lovely green. After a few minutes, the plant had restored vigor. Fu stood up and realized a crowd of people had gathered, watching him. Murmuring approval and amazement, people went on their way, but the word spread through the town of Fu's magical abilities.

"Eventually, tidings of the strange and unusual happenings in Zacát and the boy named Tung Fu reached the provincial capital, nestled in a valley several mountains of hard travel away. Whenever something truly auspicious becomes known to people of money and power, the promise of additional wealth and influence cannot be resisted. So it was that an ostentatious procession from the capital made its way to Zacát. A shepherd, his flock munching on the valley's lush grass, was casually watching the clouds that daily roll up into the pasture, when the pageantry from the capital materialized out of the mist and into the Dragon Valley. The governor of the province with his advisors, wealthy companions, and a phalanx of armed guards behind them marched up to the shepherd. The shepherd, a simple man, was overwhelmed by the entourage and quickly told them what they wanted to know, pointing the way to the house of Tung Mâh.

"Tung Mâh was not so easily intimidated. She stood placidly as the governor and the captain of his guard approached her front door. News of the governor's arrival had spread quickly throughout Zacát, and Mayor Memo with a group of townspeople rushed quickly to Mâh's home. The governor offered a perfunctory greeting to Mâh, then proceeded with the reason for his visit. 'It has come to our attention that your son has unusual abilities. There was some nonsense about dragons attending his birth, but my sources indicate that a sage has been born. It is our decision that your son would prosper and be of great benefit to the province by being under the tutelage of the wise masters of the capital city. Surely you can see the advantage this is for your son, rather than wasting his talent in this quaint little town.'

"The word 'quaint' oozed with condescension, which annoyed Mâh, and she was about to answer the governor, when Fu stepped out and walked up to the entourage. Fu's intense eyes focused on the governor and he said calmly, 'I thank you for your kind offer, but my place is here in the Dragon Valley and with the people of Zacat.'

"The look from Fu caused the governor to gasp as his mind inexplicitly opened inwardly to the truth of who he was, his prejudices and pretensions, and the arrogance and emptiness that was his life. He was stunned into silence as he began to see the beauty that was the Dragon Valley. It was the captain of the guard who reacted, roughly grabbing Fu by his thin shoulders, binding him with a rope, and throwing him to the ground. Mâh showed no reaction, but

Mayor Memo and the townspeople shouted in outrage, which muted when the guards pointed weapons at them.

"The captain looked disdainfully down at Fu and growled, 'You are coming with us, boy!' A puzzled expression twitched across his eyes as Fu calmly drew two mice in the dirt with his toes. 'What the ...?' the captain exclaimed as two mice materialized out of the ground and rapidly gnawed through the rope, freeing Fu. Everyone jumped back in astonishment and screamed in amazement — everyone except Mâh, standing unmoved, tranquil and smiling.

"Fu took off running toward the Dragon Valley. The captain and his men regained their composure and started off after the boy. Fu was fleet, his feet barely touching the grass as he ran toward Wildman, who was standing calmly, waiting for him in front of the stone statues called the Protectors. Fu stopped behind Wildman, and the captain and the guards pulled up short. Abbot Basil and the monks, who ran down the hill toward them, stopped as well. Wildman slowly raised one palm toward the aggressors, and with a small vibration of his hand sent the men sprawling.

As they attempted to regain their feet, they were shocked to see the wind spin as the wild man, with long, unkempt hair and beard, rose off the ground. Black clouds swirled in the darkened sky above. Torrential rain and lightning thundered upon the valley. Within the whirling wind, all could see a transformation happening. As the clouds cleared and the wind abated, the mysterious man known as Wildman was now an enormous, majestic azure dragon, his fierce, powerful eyes glaring threateningly at the guardsmen, who were shakily brandishing their weapons in useless gestures. The captain looked up to see, sitting high on the shoulders of the blue dragon, the boy, Fu.

"Abbot Basil fell as his knees buckled under him with the sudden comprehension of who stood before him. In a hoarse whisper he said, 'Dàmo Lung.' Then, more forcefully, he acknowledged to all the monks, 'Damo Lung has returned!'

"The azure dragon Dàmo Lung, with Tung Fu on his back, turned royally to Abbot Basil and nodded his head. The abbot and all the monks deeply bowed their respect to the dragon — as did Mayor Memo and the people of the town.

"Abbot Basil thought, no, not returned, for Dàmo Lung was always here watching over the town — just in human form. The abbot caught movement from the corner of his eye, turned, and was horrified to see the captain, with his men following, charge at the dragon. Dàmo Lung's mouth was open in a terrifying scowl, his whiskers and beard whipping about in the escalating storm, the bluish pearl on top of his head scintillating with power, and his eyes burning with such intensity that everyone averted their faces. As the captain lurched to thrust his spear into Dàmo's belly, from the dragon's scowling mouth a hot flame of bluish fire spewed forth amid a spray of water to engulf the captain — and to everyone's astonishment, the captain was no more. Dàmo, with Fu still mounted, released a deafening, banging-clanging roar, and with whipping wind and rain, he hurled the guardsmen into the mountain ravine; they were not to be seen again.

"As quickly as the turmoil began, it was over. Dàmo Lung's fury abated, but he stayed in his true dragon form. Fu slid down from the dragon and walked calmly over to the governor and his remaining attendants. His mother joined him. Mayor Memo and the townspeople gathered around, as did Abbot Basil and the monks. Dàmo watched quietly. Mâh stood serenely at Fu's side as he looked up at the governor. The governor, all the arrogance gone from his eyes, looked down at the boy.

"Fu smiled and said: 'There is a radiant consciousness when one is harmonized with the totality of nature. You know this now, don't you?'

"The governor slowly nodded his head, smiled back at Fu, and answered: 'Yes, my Sage, I do.' The governor turned to Dàmo and bowed his respect. The townspeople and monks stirred and began mumbling as the significance of the governor's words and action became clear — Tung Fu was their Sage and Dàmo Lung was their guardian dragon.

"Dàmo turned and regally walked down the Dragon Valley into the cloudy mist. Mâh put her arm around her son's shoulders and gaily spoke to everyone present: 'Good! Now, let's all have lunch together here on the grass, in the shade of our Protectors.' "

Dragon Mother shifted her weight back from the ledge and pivoted to face me. "How did you enjoy that story, David? It had a happy ending."

"I did enjoy the story, but this can't be the end, for Tung Fu is just a boy. What happens after that?"

Dragon Mother's laughter tinkled like copper coins. "Tung Fu lived to be a man famously old with a kind of wisdom unknown in this Age; but his spirit stayed young and adventurous, always reveling in the beauty of nature and the fulfilled life of a free mind. When he realized it was his time for transformation, he climbed upon the back of his father, Dàmo Lung, for one last ride into the clouds and beyond. For several generations after him, the Tung family served Zacát and the province as sages and companions to their protector, the azure dragon Dàmo Lung.

"David, do you think these are fabricated stories? Just legends? These stories are true. I am telling them to you to help you cultivate a broader and more flexible view of reality. If you are to go further in your development, you will need to open your mind to the limitless possibilities that exist in the universe — a universe infused with magic, creativity, and love."

Dog Berry 2

Red Dragon in a Tidal Wave

8

The Celestial Dragons

"The piercing chill I feel:
my dead wife's comb, in our bedroom,
under my heel ..."

The Sudden Chillness, Taniguchi Buson

It was three moons until another visit with Li-Dan, and the beach was moving into its most glorious month of October. The air was still warm to the skin, yet an intermittent chill swirled in on a breeze, diminishing the humidity and clarifying the light. The ocean, always lagging the air, was warm; the languid waves of the summer now churned with vigor and excitement. To play in the surf was exhilarating — to ride a swell as it peeled over was to experience the intoxication of surrendering to primal power.

I painted the waves tumbling upon the sand, usually with someone observing the grace of that moment. Meditating in the charged air with the breakers' soothing rumble accompanying my body rhythms added a freshness and tranquil power to my contemplation. As the autumn spilled into winter, I grew increasingly excited about visiting with Li-Dan again. On the ninth full moon, I walked briskly to the turtle dune for our rendezvous. The moon would not peek over the ocean until later in the night, but I settled on the white, crystalline sand as the light began to fade and the clouds turned mauve and gray.

As the meditative breathing technique slowed and calmed my heart, I heard a soft shuffling in the sand. I opened one eye and peered toward the sound. Waddling along was a brown pelican that plopped down beside me. Puzzled, I turned to look at him. Brown pelicans typically roost farther up the beach on pilings where the river empties into the ocean. When the pelican looked at me with his eyes twinkling, I was startled: "Oh! Li-Dan ... You are a pelican tonight!"

"Yes, what do you think? Do you like it?"

"Honestly, Li-Dan, as a pelican, you lack the regal stride and fierceness of your dragon self. The pelican-you walks awkwardly, and you are a little podgy with a bizarre beak and a floppy pouch. Nothing wrong with your pelican look, just not the magnificence of a dragon."

Li-Dan the pelican stood up on his short legs with wide-webbed feet and shuffled in front of me. A mischievous grin lit up his bird face. How, I thought, is he able to make facial expressions without a face and talk without lips?

"David, you have lived at the beach for many years. Have you ever seen a pelican on the wing above the water?"

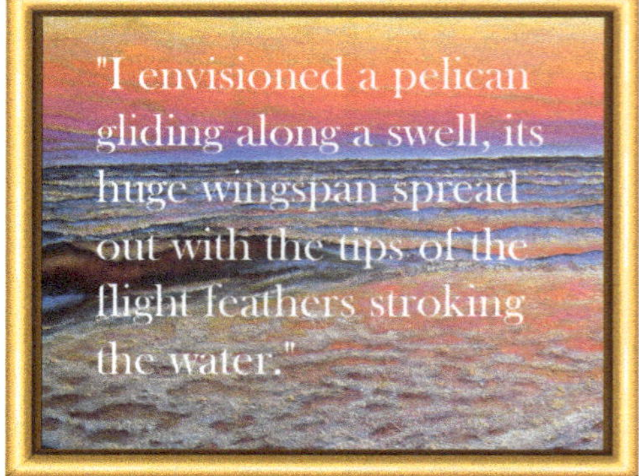

Many times, I thought, and as I stared out over the darkening water, I envisioned a pelican gliding along a swell, its huge wingspan spread out with the tips of the flight feathers stroking the water. The podgy body was elegantly streamlined in flight, its head perched majestically on top and the long beak slicing through the wind, as it rode the air currents. The grandeur of pelicans in flight always left me in awe. Then I had another vision of the pelican as hunter, circling the ocean on the updrafts looking for fish, then suddenly folding its gigantic wings and plunging down like a missile into the water, only to pop back up and float on that podgy body while the salt water drained out the beak, its dinner in the floppy pouch.

I refocused my gaze upon Li-Dan, who was studying me with a smirk. He asked, "Do you understand now?"

I smiled and nodded, "I understand." I added, "When anything operates in accordance with its innate nature, a power comes into play revealing its beauty and vitality."

"Good, David, and when anyone acts, thinks, and feels in harmony with the spiritual rhythm, then body, mind, and spirit balance, unite, and flow into wholeness. The primordial forces of magic, creativity, and love are merged in that wholeness, so that the spiritual and the material are balanced and a holistic understanding of one's relationship to the rest of creation is realized. Life is lived in its most effortless and perfect expression."

"Soaring instead of waddling," I said.

"Unless waddling is your most perfect expression," mused Li-Dan.

Li-Dan's tone lightened as he sat back down beside me. "I understand that the Dragon Mother told you the story of Tung Fu. What did you think of Tung Fu? Did you have a chance to meet him?"

"Meet him? You mean he is in the In-Between?"

"Of course he is, but he resides on a high valley in the distance through the mist, so I suppose there was no opportunity to see him."

"See him? Li-Dan, the only person I have seen in the In-Between is the Dragon Mother, and although the In-Between is hauntingly alluring, as is she, it is also desolate."

Li-Dan the pelican scratched his head with his wing and thoughtfully muttered, "Well, the In-Between is more populous than you might think, but the Dragon Mother is working with you, and she has her own ways. I know her desire to help you prepare for the new Age is considerable."

"Wait! What? Li-Dan! Please, I keep hearing about the Ages, and yet I have no understanding what you or the Dragon Mother are talking about. And why does she want to help me?"

"She wants to help you, as do I, for that is what we do. You are not unique, and you are not alone. I will address your curiosity about the Ages, because now is the time for us to talk about the celestial dragons."

I turned to face Li-Dan. He was sitting there with his large, flat feet splayed out in front of him, the tips of the webbed toes flicking sand into the air. The silliness of it made it difficult for me to stay focused on this serious conversation, but I was talking with a pelican after all.

Li-Dan began, "If you remember, in our last conversation we talked about the earthly dragons. I told you that there were also celestial dragons and spiritual dragons, and that they had different origins and purposes. The discussion on spiritual dragons is for another time. Tonight, we will discuss celestial dragons and the Ages of Humankind.

"Earthly dragons were supernaturally created and have supernatural powers, but they are not divine. They are of the earth; however, their supernatural powers are related to the control of the primal elements of fire, water, earth, and air; thus, they can influence the forces of life to the benefit or detriment of humankind.

"From the singularity, and moving with the intent of the Creator, come forth the primordial forces, existing throughout the universe as the forces of magic, creativity, and love, to execute the purposes of the Source. The present world of humankind is neither the first nor the only world in existence. Before this world was created, there existed many others. Apart from this cosmos, there are numerous other cosmic systems with the primordial forces exerting their influences. Each cosmos and each world exist in a state of duality, and as such, and by necessity, each has a beginning and an end.

"In this world, David, it is deemed that there shall be nine Ages of Humankind. Why nine? That is not a question for us to know. I will say the number nine is a holy symbol, a multiplication of the number three, which represents heaven, light, and truth; therefore, nine is the symbol of immutable truth — for truth never changes. Did this symbolism come to us through the primordial forces? I do not know, but it is known that each Age lasts for approximately 10,800 years. We are currently approaching the end of the seventh Age.

"When the time is imminent for the close of an Age, the primordial forces coalesce as the spiritual force, activating an immeasurable energy force. Through the influence of the magical and creative forces, this massive energy source condenses into the form of a celestial dragon. Celestial dragons are the supreme and most sacred of the three forms of dragons. This divinely created dragon becomes the Celestial Dragon of Destruction, the agent for ending an Age of Humankind.

"The earthly dragons are aware of the approach of an Age's end and go into hibernation to preserve their strength in preparation for the work they have to do. The stupendous Celestial Dragon of Destruction, as a divine messenger, is sent earthward to call the earthly dragons out of hibernation and into action. The Celestial Dragon with seven terrifying heads is fully a hundred miles long, and streaks into the earth's atmosphere, traveling faster than the earth, overtaking it in its rotation. Each of the dragon's seven mouths shoots out gigantic bolts of lightning, destroying whole sections of the earth. The body of the immense beast, traveling at an incredible speed, begins to glow. With the increasing intensity of light, the horrified inhabitants of the earth futilely run around in a panic searching for a place of safety. The Celestial Dragon begins to glow a hundred times brighter than the sun, and eyes that look upon it are blinded.

"Before crashing into the ocean, the Celestial Dragon of Destruction issues forth a roaring gardyloo that awakens the earthly dragons from their lairs to begin their work, bursting eardrums around the world. When the Celestial Dragon plunges into the ocean, steam hisses up in massive columns and a tidal wave of continental-swallowing size blasts out in all directions. The earthly dragons, with their control of the primal elements, bring about catastrophes of fires, floods, and hurricanes. Fierce fireballs are vomited upon the earth, and heavy rains fall until the forests and mountains are covered by the rising waters. The earth trembles, the seas are driven out of their beds, and mountains erupt from the earth. Life everywhere is ruined, and traces of the old Age are obliterated. The world is consumed, only to be shaped anew."

"Damn, Li-Dan!" I stammered. "Oops, maybe I shouldn't say that?"

"No. Damn is right, David. It sounds horrible to you, I know, but you should not be a mumpsimus about this."

"Mumpsimus! Li-Dan, please! Now is not the time for word games. What you just told me is horrifying."

"I understand you are disturbed, but it is the proper word. The Dragon Mother and I are helping you to re-evaluate your view of reality. Humans become ingrained with the habit of thinking only about themselves, as if the whole universe, the whole of creation, is for them and revolves around them. Nature is thought to be expendable if it benefits them. The Ages provide the opportunity for humankind to rise above this egocentric obsession. Although each Age develops differently, the same opportunity is afforded for individuals to be in harmony with the intent and consciousness of the singularity. Do you have a sense of what I am saying?"

"I suppose, but humans have self-awareness, which separates them from the rest of life forms. Doesn't that afford them a unique place in the creation?"

"David, can you really say for certain that only humans have self-awareness? Understand that all life is imbued with the exact same life force, originating from the same source. In that sense, all life is the same, all life is connected, and all life comprises a whole. You may think this is goggledygook, but why is the life of a human more precious than the life of an insect? There is only one life in this world, David! Every person is nothing more than a miniscule aspect of it."

Well, that shut me up for a while. I sat quietly for a long time. Li-Dan the pelican did the same. In the cold night air, the moon overhead shone with clarity, casting shadows around Li-Dan and me. A chill from the night-dampened sand penetrated my clothing. I shuddered, whether from the cold or from the revelation about the Ages, I did not know. I looked into Li-Dan's beady bird eyes and confessed, "I am beginning to understand, but I think I require more time."

"Of course, David, but it might help if I tell you about the formation of the current Age, the Seventh Age." Li-Dan, seeing me shiver, opened his enormous pelican mouth and exhaled dragon warmth over me. Cozying in on the sand, I sighed and tried to control my apprehension of what was to follow.

Ethereal Faces Floating Freely

White Dragon in Red Sky

9

The Seventh Age of Humankind

With love one is fearless
With moderation one is abundant
With humility one can fill the highest position
Now if one is fearless but has not love
abundant but has no moderation
rises up but has no humility
Surely he is doomed.

Tao Te Ching, Verse 67, Lao Tzu

long night ensued, but finally, the Dragon Mother's and Li-Dan's mysteries had answers. Li-Dan the pelican puffed up his pouch and slowly hissed out air as he began in his deep pelican voice. "Let's start with the destruction of the reigning civilization at the end of the Sixth Age."

"At that time, an island continent in the Atlantic Ocean was the center of world civilization. Formed from towering volcanic mountains, the island had vast, fertile plains where grains were cultivated and animals domesticated. The island people were a tall, well-proportioned, bronze-skinned race. As their civilization advanced and flourished, their influence extended abroad to the east and west, making them the major world power.

"The people thrived on this enormous island with its many springs, rivers, and surrounding seas; and they lived in harmony with the dragons, for they understood the blessings or destructions the dragons could bestow. The population respected the dragons for their supernatural powers

77

and entreated the dragons to send the nourishing rain. Consequently, this civilization grew and prospered.

"As the centuries passed, the people advanced their civilization. They developed a complex writing system, along with a knowledge of astronomy and mathematics. They erected great buildings and created beautiful art. With each advancement, the rulers and priests became bloated with pride, setting themselves above the dragons. Eventually, malice festered as the people grew violent and greedy. The dragons hid in inaccessible mountain caverns and in the fathomless sea depths, gathering strength and awaiting the call into activity.

"Around 10,000 B.C., almost 1,500 years before the time of destruction, the dragons were seen no more. Civilizations of the Sixth Age forgot the reality of dragons as they moved into the realm of myth and legend. The few people who still believed in the ancients' wisdom understood what the dragons' disappearance meant and began to prepare for their own salvation.

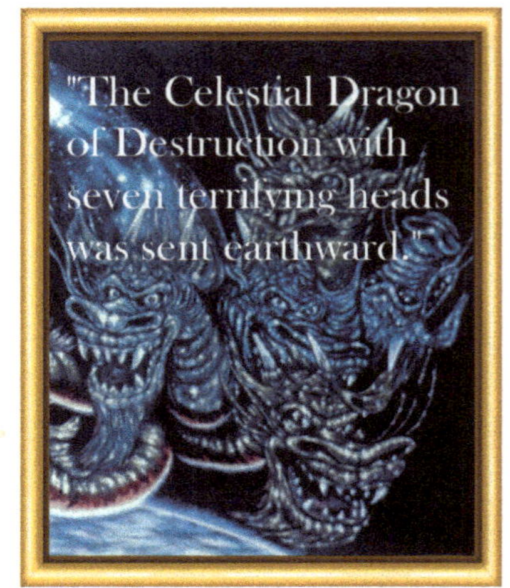

"Sometime around the year 8500 B.C., prodigies heralded the end time. Earthquakes, floods, and other natural disasters increased. The earth's temperature altered rapidly, disrupting the stability of life. Planetary alignment gave the final signal, as the sun and moon changed their colors. The Celestial Dragon of Destruction with seven terrifying heads was sent earthward.

"Streaking for the island nation in the Atlantic Ocean and issuing the thunderous cry to call the earthly dragons, the Celestial Dragon crashed and pierced the thinnest region of the earth's crust — the Atlantic Ridge. A low rumbling preceded a sudden blast of thunder of the enormous explosion. Shock waves raced across the earth. People all over the world were thrown to the ground. Buildings tumbled into heaps. The sea bottom burst open as the earth's crust was shattered. The island with its great and powerful civilization disintegrated, the land seething before being engulfed by the sea, all life extinguished.

"In the midst of whirlwinds and catastrophic thunderstorms, the roused dragons all over the earth rose into activity after nearly two thousand years of hibernation. Assuming tremendous size, the dragons churned ever upward in tornado spouts that reached into the upper atmosphere. Thousands of dragons raised mighty winds and vomited fierce squalls.

"The devastated earth heaved and fractured. Volcanoes retched fire and ash; the ash formed a colossal soup of doom the size of continents that moved with the dragons to cover the earth. Violent lightning bolts, tornadoes, and hurricanes of unimaginable ferocity preceded the torrential rain, so saturated with muck from the ash that winged creatures were unable to escape, sucked into the maelstrom. On anguished seas, dead bodies rode monstrous waves. The Age of the Bronze People was over.

"Gradually the rains ceased, and the waters receded. It was now the beginning of the new Age. The Celestial Dragon upon impact caused a shift in the pole of rotation, so that the earth's axis became more oblique, creating seasons on the earth. The earthly dragons began establishing the new world structure. Clouds thinned as the shadow of darkness lifted from the land. This occurred everywhere except northern Europe, where something special took place. Black and red dragons swirled in large circular motions over Europe, piling clouds of dust and debris into dense, towering barriers of the sun. Considerable quantities of moisture collected in these oppressive clouds, leaving the land beneath a dimmed, misty, cold, and damp place. Europe was a world of endless night, lit by a dim glow, shrouded in gloom for over two thousand years.

"Without the sun's radiant power, only a few species of moss, lichen, and plants were able to adapt themselves. Reindeer and musk ox that fed on these plants managed to survive. The few people remaining barely managed a meager existence by hunting, herding, and fishing. This epoch of darkness and bare subsistence halted the progression of civilization here, and it was the incubation period of a new race of people. In the 2,000-year period of dark mist, through generation after generation, the people gradually lost their bronzed color and became pallid. Here developed the mutant white race — the race of humans with pigment-deficient skin.

"In China and Asia, dragons are considered beneficent beings, this viewpoint going back to the beginning of the Age. Blue and yellow dragons with tornadoes and thunderstorms moved from the Atlantic across Europe and northern Asia and down to the region known now as China. Even though the dragons produced considerable destruction and death, they deposited rich soil formed from the volcanic ash and marine ooze. This soil was the famous yellow earth of China, one of the most fertile soils in the world. The yellow and blue dragons gave the people a gift to help the survivors rebuild civilization in a bountiful land. From the beginning, the people venerated the noble dragons for the blessings bestowed upon them, not only the loess, but assistance in developing language, art, and philosophy.

"Into the north of Africa, hordes of white dragons with whirlwinds of intense heat scorched their way slowly across the once fertile land, burning a path across the continent. The ground dried up with dust and sand agitating into huge, orange clouds, miles high, churning and blowing for hundreds of years. Massive dunes formed and re-formed around the bodies of the dead. The continent's northern part became an arid wasteland, as the white dragons slowly advanced into the Arabian Peninsula and into Mongolia. Everywhere the land was transformed into an extensive, forbidding wasteland, sun-seared and wind-scoured, waterless and endless. The intense sunlight induced protective changes for the people struggling to survive, as their skin darkened to withstand the torrid environment.

"The tall, bronze-skinned people of the Sixth Age had migrated and established their civilization in all directions from their Atlantic island. Those who ranged and lived in what is now the Americas survived much of the destruction that afflicted the rest of the world. As remnants, they embody a continuity of the Ages, for their civilization carried into the new Age a residue of the truth that all life is connected as one.

"As it relates to the beginning of this Seventh Age, David, the record is abundant. All the ancient civilizations have stories about dragons and a colossal destruction. The ancient world knew that the dragon was king of the creation and had special powers, for the dragon became the emblem of royalty and the symbol of greatness everywhere. Even in Europe, where the dragon was looked upon as evil, its image was used in heraldic ornaments. The Teutonic tribes who invaded and settled in England bore the effigies of dragons on their shields and banners. The dragon image on early Germanic helmets was considered magical. The dragon was considered the national standard of the Celts, as well as the Romans.

"In Ethiopia, South Guinea, and Abyssinia, there are many stories of dragons, and the seven-headed Dragon of Destruction is found in the myths and legends of Japan, Scotland, Cambodia, India, Persia, western Asia, east Africa, and the Mediterranean area. Dragons feature in the legends of Egypt, Greece, India, Babylonia, Assyria, Indonesia, and the Americas.

"The dragon standard was adopted by the emperor of Constantinople from the Assyrians, and in Babylonia, it was an object of worship. The Hebrews' descriptions of cherubim and seraphim, orders of angels, are portrayals of dragons. In China, the five-clawed yellow dragon defined the emperor. In Japan and Korea, the dragon was a symbol of beneficence and identified with emperors and kings. Even today, David, everybody in the world has notions about dragons, although mostly fantasy, but the mystery of the dragons has never passed away. Why? Because the reality of dragons is ingrained in the collective consciousness of all humankind.

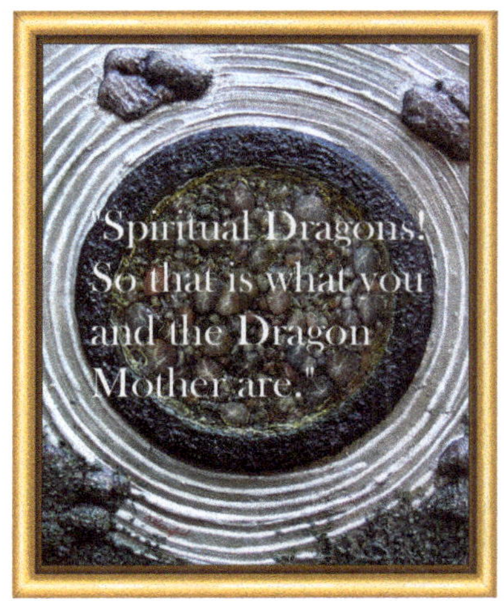

"The forces of life, constituting the supernatural powers of the dragons, are impersonal — humans are of no consequence. The idea of dragons as evil comes from the duality nature of humankind. Humankind, relegated to an inferior place to dragons, sought to extend its domination over them, as well as the rest of the creation. This incessant struggle evolved into the eternal contest of people against the forces of nature and their two-fold self. This is the damnation for humans, and the only salvation is for everyone to strive for an enlightened state by subjugating their egos, desires, and fears, and aligning themselves with the spiritual force of the universe. We have spoken of this, David, and those who have completed the journey can reveal the way to others, but spiritual enlightenment is an individual endeavor. Facilitation on this journey is the mission of the spiritual dragons."

To put emphasis on his revelation about "spiritual dragons," Li-Dan eyeballed me, measuring my reaction.

My reaction was total fascination. "Spiritual dragons! So that is what you and the Dragon Mother are. You told me that you were something different from an earthly dragon, and that confused me. You are a red spiritual dragon, and the Dragon Mother is a yellow spiritual dragon, right?"

"I can see that you are flabbergasted, David, and not to bloviate, but yes, we are spiritual dragons. The Dragon Mother wants to be the one to talk with you about the spiritual dragons, so I will say no more. Meet me here the next full moon, and I will relate the miraculous story of the dancer Lau Shen and her transformation into the Dragon Mother."

"Absolutely, I can meet you here … especially to hear about the Dragon Mother!" I said a little too enthusiastically. Li-Dan scrunched one of his pelican eyes curiously as he tilted his head to study me.

"What! Okay, I am intrigued by her," I countered defensively. Lowering my voice, I bashfully muttered, "She has a bewitching way about her."

"That she does, and when you have heard her story, you will understand why. I will see you again soon."

A northeaster had picked up from the ocean. Li-Dan opened his pelican wings and, after skipping a few steps, was airborne, gliding effortlessly over the waves, riding the wind into the distance. I walked home down the beach, engrossed once more in thought about Li-Dan's revelations, already excited about the next conversation.

Pink and Green on the Pond

Black Dragon Catches Sparrow

10

The Pink Dragons of the Aurora

Ono no Komachi

ith my mind reeling over apocalyptic visions, painting was difficult for a few days, but finally, I purged this discord by executing a small painting called "Rise and Fall." In this painting I put the energies of line, mass, and color into a rhythmical relation to animate the despair I felt. As the time approached to meet with Li-Dan, the excitement of hearing the Dragon Mother story overpowered my distress. On the appointed day, I woke early and enjoyed the morning meditation in the studio. By the late afternoon, I decided to stroll to the turtle dune and embrace the ocean breeze and meditate until Li-Dan's arrival.

As I approached the secluded dune, I spotted a tiny old man walking at the surf's edge. He was struggling as the waves washed over his sandals, sinking them into the water-softened sand — obviously not a beach person.

"Take your sandals off and merge with the energy of the water," I muttered to myself, but then I realized who it was.

Bald head with shoulder-length, white hair circling his shiny dome, drooping, white mustache attached to a flowing goatee — this could only be one person. "Li-Dan, you came as you! But why the T-shirt and shorts? Where's your robe?"

"What did you think, David? That I would walk the beach in a robe? This clothing is infinitely more comfortable and practical. Also, I did not want to be mistaken for a gaberlunzie."

"No, no, that would never do, but take off your sandals, Li-Dan. We walk the beach barefooted. I like your new look as Lao Tzu ... which, I suppose, is your old look, but it is a good look, nonetheless."

"Well, I was quite a bit, uh, rounder, when I was Lao Tzu, but the wonder of transformation is that I can make modifications. A trimmer middle suits me better, don't you think?"

"I do. You are quite striking," I chuckled. "Shall we sit? I am excited to hear your story about the Dragon Mother. It's a true story, right?"

"As true as I could glean, but you know, there is always a storyteller's prerogative — I can embellish here and there. Settle in, for this is a wonderful story of a little lost girl, who became the Dragon Mother. As you know, I am of this Age, although from some time ago," said Li-Dan. "The Dragon Mother is from a previous Age; what Age, I do not know. I don't think anyone knows; no one has the indiscretion to ask. She has been a part of the In-Between for an eternity."

My brow wrinkled in bewilderment. "The In-Between has never been fully explained to me. Is it part of the duality? Where is it ... what is it?"

"It is difficult for someone from a duality existence to fully grasp the nature of the In-Between. It is a physical space and a state of being, and time is very flexible within it. The In-Between is tenuously attached to this reality and has its own vibrational frequency, pitched to an impossibly high degree, and with an odd, attendant rhythm. This rhythm produces a fluctuating pattern that is revealed as the In-Between.

"The primordial forces empower the In-Between, and since they originate from non-duality but operate within the duality, the In-Between exists in between perfection and imperfection, complete and incomplete, permanent and impermanent — in between the exuberance of residing in the spiritual light or living a shadowy, material existence. Does that satisfy your questions, David?"

"No, Li-Dan, it doesn't, but as you indicated before, it is only fully comprehended when experienced. Since I have been there, I have a sense of what you said. With more meditation, I am sure I will realize a more holistic understanding." A thought came to mind about the Dragon Mother. "Does the Dragon Mother ever leave the In-Between and visit this world like you?"

"Do you remember when she told you the story about Hana, and you asked about the dog, Gaea?" I nodded. "Gaea was the Dragon Mother safeguarding Hana. She loved Hana. That story was true. Does that surprise you?"

I shook my head. "No, that does not surprise me at all."

"Splendiferous! Now allow me to tell you the story of a little girl named Lau-Lau, and how she became the Dragon Mother. I call this story 'The Pink Dragons of the Aurora.' "

"There are no pink dragons, Li-Dan," I contradicted.

"That's right, David, and that is part of the wonder of the story."

"The Ages share similarities due to the basic human makeup and the intrinsic nature of the universe. Humans seek out their needs, and civilizations develop accordingly. The cosmos and this world are bound by duality, thus there is a cyclical continuity to the Ages. Within each Age, civilizations develop along the human goal-oriented nature, but always present are the opportunities for people to merge and flow with the primordial forces, and thus to experience spiritual perfection, bestowing upon themselves the blessings of freedom and happiness.

"The woman to become known as Lau-Shen came into the world with an inborn affinity for the creative rhythm. Later it became apparent she also possessed an aptitude for the magical rhythm. What she lacked was the ability to know love. This was not surprising, since she did not remember her parents, and she was very young when she was found alone, dancing on the streets of Leelan, a city along the Golden River.

"The Golden River was part of a large river system that wandered from the headwaters of the far northern White Mountains, with their volcanic crater lakes, through limestone cliffs of the tall hills of pine, maple, and elm, and onto the flat, yellow-mud delta before emptying into the Golden Sea. As the river rushed to the sea, loess was gathered in the churning, yellowed water.

At the delta, the water deposited this rich soil, providing Leelan with a booming agricultural economy.

"The city of Leelan sprawled across the delta's yellow flats to the river and climbed onto the higher ground of a basin formed by bluffs on three sides. The city had a humid, subtropical climate with seasonal variations of temperature and rain. Summers were hot, humid, and wet; and while the winters could be cold, the farmers grew two crops a year. The Golden River was navigable to the city with a constant influx of ships, making Leelan a prosperous port of call. This also meant that a wealthy merchant class arose with the means and desires to be entertained.

"A glamorous entertainment center emerged to accommodate the demands for pleasure from both the wealthy citizens and the ship merchants. Walled off from the rest of the city, The Rose, as the center was called, became its own separate enclave for the beauty-obsessed elite. There were courtesans, to be sure, but music, dancing, and singing entertained the clients of The Rose. Renowned actors performed skits, and poets recited. This burgeoning profession of paid entertainment, overseen by dowagers, cultivated extensive apprenticeship programs to teach promising youths. The young, dancing child plunged from mud between her toes into this world.

"Nothing was known about the little girl, except she was found dancing in the mud by Po Agg, a boy a few years older who was training in dance and singing at The Rose. How she had survived alone on the streets of Leelan was a mystery. When Po brought the girl before Madam Zu San, the dowager's eyes widened, for she saw something immediately in the girl's walk. Grace emanated in her every movement. Her body moved in harmony as one, no wasted or jerky motions. She was as fluid as the gentle breezes that flowed from the river. Madam Zu San had seen this only rarely in professional dancers after years of training. Never in a child.

"Madam Zu San was an imposing, matronly woman. Although she was strict and demanding with her students and dancers, she was not unkind. Of all the dowagers in The Rose, Madam Zu San possessed the keenest business acumen, becoming as wealthy as her patrons. She was tall with light brown hair riddled in gray (she called it silver) tied back to her shoulders. She leaned slightly on a hefty walking stick, made of black ironwood, ornately carved as a dragon rising. With the walking stick in her hand, the dragon's black head perched imposingly above her grip, she strode assertively about her domain. For this reason, Madam Zu San was commonly called Madam Three-Legs. This moniker was never uttered in her presence, for Madam Three-Legs had the reputation of using the dragon head to chasten imprudent behavior.

"Po Agg watched as Madam Zu San locked eyes with the ragamuffin. "What is your name, child?" she asked in a voice that intimidated Po but had no effect on the girl, who studied the madam impassively and responded nonchalantly, 'Lau-Lau.' The utter detachment in Lau-Lau's demeanor intrigued Madam Zu San, for she knew that the girl's natural dispassion in combination with an elusively sensual dancing style would elicit profound desires from her clientele. Lau-Lau will be famous, the madam thought, and I will be very wealthy. Madam Zu San smiled down at Lau-Lau and asserted, 'Girl, I am going to help you become the greatest dancer ever!' Lau-Lau responded in her cool manner, 'Yes, that is what I will be.'

"That is what happened. Madam Zu San was very attentive to Lau-Lau's training over the next few years. She provided the finest instructors in The Rose for her, but Lau-Lau quickly surpassed them all. Lau-Lau's mastery of technique reached perfection and went beyond, tapping into a source that none of her teachers could understand. When she danced, it was as if a mystical force moved her with a powerful and elegant rhythm, the energies of her movements interacting with the energies around her. Lau-Lau's dynamic rhythm of creativity irresistibly resonated with the creative rhythm of the universe. The beauty and intensity of her dance entranced patrons whose desire to dance with her overwhelmed them. The young dancing child, Lau-Lau, developed magical powers of enchantment in her dancing, and became known as Lau Shen, 'Spiritual Lau.' Her dances revealed, then subdued, the sorrows, vanity, and anger of mortality, allowing the beholders to transcend imperfection briefly and sense the grace of spiritual perfection.

"Lau Shen's unusual beauty became legendary throughout Leelan and beyond. Lau Shen was above average height, her torso and limbs long and supple, her bronze-colored skin luscious and smooth, and her hair ebony and very curly. Prominent cheekbones framed wide, full lips and long, dark lashes intensified her golden amber eyes. The deep, rich tones of her voice enhanced her seductive demeanor. She became the epitome of feminine beauty in Leelan.

"Suitors came in abundance, for all men wanted to be with her. Lau Shen had never experienced love, did not know how to love, and had no feelings of love within her, but she soon learned how to manipulate her coquettish control over men. Because of Lau Shen's high status and wealth, Madam Zu San allowed her to live independently, her romantic life her own. And many romantic affairs she had, but never did she love. She toyed with men, used them, and her reputation for cruel treatment of her lovers was widely known; still, men avidly sought her affections.

"Po Agg grew tall and handsome. He danced with masculine strength and power, the perfect foil for Lau Shen, and so they often danced together as partners. All the years they were together as children training, he watched over her. With his goofy sense of humor, Po was the only one who made her genuinely smile. He was her only companion and friend as the years of training went by, but never was he able to pierce the shroud of detachment that wrapped around her.

"Po watched the parade of lovers walk in and out of Lau Shen's life and witnessed the heartless games she played, but still he loved her. He knew his love was genuine, for he fully understood her essence. Po knew what was missing was her ability to love, to receive and give it freely. If he could reveal to her the nature of genuine love, if he gave his love to her purely with no expectations, perhaps, it would find a home within her, and she would finally embrace love.

"Po Agg was a young man, so naturally his love was rife with passion. On a cool night, Po and Lau Shen were performing a particularly sensuous dance. The patrons, raucously expressing their pleasure, elevated the finale to a frenzy. After Lau Shen and Po Agg executed the final movement entwined in each other's arms, wet with perspiration and breathing heavily, they walked together out into the night air, away from the crowd. Po's feelings were at a fever pitch, his breathing still hard and fast. He could contain his passionate love for Lau Shen no longer. He professed his love for her. Lau Shen had feelings for Po, not love, but they had been together for many years.

" 'Po, I feel no love for you, or for anyone. I like you, and I think we are excellent dancing together, but there is no love.'

"In his chest, Po felt a strange ache, and his stomach knotted, but what Lau Shen said, Po already knew. He swallowed down the emotions that were engulfing him. Taking a deep breath, he looked into her mesmerizing, golden eyes for a moment, and his knees weakened. Glancing up at the crescent moon, he tried to regain his composure. 'Lau-Lau,' he said, using her childhood name, 'You have a shadow within you, a void that is disconnecting you from life.

It will destroy you. No, it is destroying you. My love for you is too great for me to allow that to happen. Please let me have the honor to bestow upon you my love, for you to know what love truly is, to feel it deeply within you.'

"Lau Shen stared into Po Agg's pleading eyes, startled to realize that they were a lustrous green. He was handsome, she thought, but she was not sure what to say. How does one understand the absence of something that one never has had? Love was a concept that had no reality to her, but she did like Po, and they had been together for many years. Her only point of reference was her romantic affairs with her myriad of suitors, so consistent with her treatment of her other lovers, she cavalierly promised that if he would visit her continuously for eighty-one nights and dance for her, then she would become his lover, at least for a time.

"In his fierce passion and deep love for Lau Shen, Po was ecstatic, for he knew in his heart that his love was pure enough to lure her to embrace love. He agreed to her conditions. Every day he created a new dance, and every night he performed. Driven by his desire to show Lau Shen his love, he crafted day after day masterpieces of dance, charged with life and power, like nothing seen, even at The Rose. Po danced just for his love.

"With each night his creativity attained new heights as the creative cosmic force resonated within him ever more powerfully. The force of magic became attracted to him as well as he sought to infuse his dance creations with the allure of love and the joy of intimate connections. Inspired solely by his love for Lau Shen, the rhythm of love permeated his dancing to embody the spiritual presence of the universe. Every single night, Po Agg danced before her with ever-increasing power — power that even she did not possess. Lau Shen was stunned.

"On the eightieth night, Po Agg was at the height of his power. As he spun and turned on Lau Shen's terrace, his moistened body shimmering with the light of a gibbous moon, the air rippled and flowed with him. Lau Shen felt a humming surround her as her skin shivered. She staggered back, her heart raging in her chest, a tingling cascading through her body in sequence to Po's impassioned, rhythmic motions. Looking upon Po, an ache welled up in her chest as her emotions intensified.

"Spiraling down on one knee in front of her as he finished his eightieth dance, Po looked up into Lau Shen's tearful eyes. She gazed upon him with desire, and Po knew that he had kindled a fire in her heart. Without saying a word, he stood up and faced his love. Taking her hand, he gently raised it to his lips, and with a soft kiss, Po turned and walked silently into the moonlit night. Lau Shen was motionless for a very long time.

"The next day Lau Shen spent in feverish anticipation. Something had changed inside her. She could feel it. It was glorious and melancholic at the same time, but all that mattered to her was to see him on night eighty-one — to relish the passion of his dancing, to be alive again in the glow of his love. To tell him she returned his love. What Lau Shen desired above all else was to dance the dance of love with Po Agg.

"Po had been planning his final dance for Lau Shen for many days. It was the climax of an eighty-one-day obsession, his transcendental moment, but Po sat quietly in his room contemplating nothing. In his mind and body, the final dance was already mastered, as every dance had been before. There was something else happening that he could not explain. As he danced, he found himself an observer, watching himself move with a power that far surpassed his abilities. His dancing was perfect, flowing with grace and power, his whole body in complete harmony with his mind and spirit, and connected with something he did not comprehend fully. He was not just dancing — he was dance.

"Every year, the city of Leelan held a festival called the Dragon Boat Festival, which originally was in honor of the local dragon, to assure the proper rains. Most of the city's people no longer believed in dragons, but tradition made it a grand celebration nonetheless. Races on the Golden River with dragon boats, long, narrow vessels with a dragon's head at the bow, were a favorite event. In the evening a procession marched through the center of Leelan with fireworks, led by a dragon constructed of wooden frames covered with paper and carried by young people, who danced along behind a child dancing backward and carrying the dragon's pearl. In his preoccupation, Po Agg forgot about the festival until he left his apartment for Lau Shen's residence. Deciding to avoid the crowded streets, he climbed up on the wall surrounding The Rose to walk around to his love. Below, The Rose and the city of Leelan were festive with colors and lights, music and dancing. Out on the river, the dragon boats were sluggishly floating with lanterns that illuminated their dazzling colors. Reflected in languid patterns on the darkened river, the light of the full moon was brilliant in the cloudless, evening sky. Po stopped walking for a moment to contemplate the serenity and beauty of the spectacle. Then, the inconceivable happened.

"As Po stared in disbelief, the river water began to swirl in ever-increasing intensity, until there was a giant whirlpool churning in the middle of the broad river. The dragon boats twisted and spun with the maelstrom, slamming into each other. People along the river started screaming and moving away from the water's edge. The evening breeze over the river roiled in sync with the water, forming a waterspout spinning up into the moonlit sky. Po was astonished when out of the water there emerged a huge, black shape, as the waterspout spun into a violent tornado. As the shape fully surfaced, Po was in shocked disbelief to realize it was a massive, black dragon. A dragon had not been seen in Leelan for eons.

"Clouds issued from the dragon's mouth, spiraling into colossal thunderheads that spat lightning down upon the river. When the black dragon reached the towering clouds, it cast a fleeting look at the tall man on the wall, then rocketed north toward the White Mountains. A powerful wind gust from the streaking dragon caught Po by surprise, spinning him to the edge of the wall. The dancer in him reacted intuitively, dropping his left shoulder to counter the cross-blow, his right leg extended out to pivot him until he was standing firmly on the wall facing the river — an exquisite move. Dancer that he was, instinctively he threw both arms into the air in a heroic finale, and to the horror of the people watching below, a thunderous lightning bolt blasted him. Po stood in stunned astonishment, arms still up in a grand gesture to his last dance, and tumbled backward into the courtyard of The Rose. Still conscious, time slowed for Po Agg; every moment as he plummeted was clear and precise. He knew he had fulfilled his mission and opened the heart of Lau Shen, his final gift of love. The irony was not lost on him, but he had saved his love. Po smiled his last smile as he hit the stone pavers. Pandemonium broke out as fellow entertainers ran to his lifeless body, a small, peculiar smile frozen on his lips.

"Lau Shen was growing apprehensive over Po's tardiness. He was never late for his time with her. Uncertainty played various scenarios in her imagination, when her awareness shifted to the uproar outside. Looking out upon the terrace, she saw people running to the compound wall. Something shivered through her mind and body, panic overtaking her as she ran with the crowd. She had heard the deafening thunderclap; everyone in Leelan had heard it, and now dread overwhelmed her.

"At the sight of the gathered crowd, Lau Shen stopped, her breath coming in short gasps. As the people became aware of Lau Shen's presence, they began to move away, so that she saw Po in his final pose. With hands clasped at her chest, head lowered in sorrow, and golden eyes swelling with tears, she moved haltingly to Po's stilled body. Dropping to her knees, tears flowed down her cheeks as she looked upon his final smile. Lau Shen leaned over and kissed the smile meant for her. Po had won her heart. Her body began to shudder uncontrollably, until a firm arm wrapped around her shoulders and drew her to her feet. Looking through her tears, Lau Shen beheld the maternal strength of Madam Zu San. Gently, the madam led her protégée away, the full moon lighting the way and casting forlorn shadows that epitomized the inconsolable pain Lau Shen felt.

"The days and weeks that followed were a blur of anguish and darkness. Lau Shen found herself walking day and night along the river, barefooted, the mud of the delta squeezing between her toes, trying in vain to walk away the pain. She could not eat. Food had no taste. She could not sleep, sweating and chilling simultaneously in her bed, her legs restless and fidgety, her body hurting as much as her mind. Unbridled emotions controlled her life; harmony and balance were gone. And still, she walked and walked, always barefooted, always in the mud — until one day, she simply walked away from The Rose and the city of Leelan.

"Time lost any meaning to Lau Shen. Weeks, months — she did not know how long she wandered. Many people throughout the province took pity, giving her food from time to time. Others, remembering her cruel treatment of her lovers, shunned her. Lau Shen did not care how she was treated or if she ate, and it showed as her once powerful and imposing dancer's body grew weak and thin, and her exquisite face gaunt, her golden eyes haunted and dull. Wandering north away from Leelan's province, with her tattered clothes and wretched appearance, she became an object of mockery and disdain. Beauty dissipated, desire for life gone, Lau Shen straggled on, mindlessly following the Golden River.

"Abbess Trishan of the Covenant of Dragons was out in the fields gathering sweet potatoes from the rich, yellow dirt. Straightening up to wipe the perspiration from her eyes, she was startled to see an emaciated creature lurching along the river path. As Abbess Trishan watched, the pathetic-looking woman, with black matted hair curling wildly and a filthy bodice hanging off bony shoulders, stumbled this way and that, until she tripped on a rock and toppled to her knees. The pitiful woman gazed upon the muddy river, then resigned to die, she slowly lowered herself prone upon the ground. Abbess Trishan was already running across the field toward her.

"When Lau Shen awoke, it was night. She was clean, dressed in a khaki-colored robe, and lying on a cot in a cave. On a small table by the cot was a wooden bowl of soup, sweet potato, she thought. Sitting beside her was a small woman, also in a khaki-colored robe, holding a smaller bowl of greenish liquid. 'Lie quietly, my dear,' she whispered, 'and drink this; it will calm you and help you to rest.' Lau Shen, weak and docile, did as she was instructed. Looking over at her savior, she beheld the most compassionate face she had ever seen. Their eyes met, and her savior smiled and slightly bobbed her head as if she had divined something. Lau Shen surrendered to a deep sleep.

"The Covenant of Dragons was an extremely old order established when dragons were prevalent upon the earth. They were devoted to understanding, documenting, and assisting dragons. The Covenant was not exactly a religion, but dragons were creatures of reverence to them, bordering on worship. No dragons had been seen in their vicinity for generations, but their devotion did not fail, for they understood what it meant for dragons to be scarce. The Covenant had a few hundred devotees, mostly women, but a few men as well. Abbess Trishan was the most knowledgeable and devoted, and with her kindheartedness she became their leader.

"The Covenant was in an area of limestone cliffs and forested hills along the river, called the Dragon Grottoes. The grottoes, or caves, had been in continual habitation for thousands of years. The caves were not natural, but were the product of continuous excavations into the limestone over the millennia. There were more than two thousand caves and niches, filled with many more thousands of carved limestone statues of dragons. Some were small, others were colossal, and most were painted richly in five-color combinations. Carved obelisks and stelae with inscriptions and reliefs adorned the open areas around the caves, as monuments to dragon milestones through the ages. The Dragon Grottoes were on both sides of the Golden River with two steep, rocky hills north of the grottoes called the Dragon's Gate that marked the entrance into the Covenant. Most residences were in the eastside caves where there was flat ground for growing crops. The westside caves with numerous pagodas along the river served as temples for study and meditation. Behind the cliffs, the hills were covered in hardwood and pine forests and were abundant in game and wildlife.

"After a few days of rest and with the constant attention of the abbess, Lau Shen stepped out of the cave and promptly fell back in. Moving from the dimness of the cave to the brilliance of the grottoes overpowered her. Thousands of huge, colorful dragon statues and carved reliefs, amid a honeycomb of caves everywhere, startled her. Abbess Trishan, expecting such a reaction, braced Lau Shen as she led her out into the morning light. The abbess walked her over to a pagoda and, sitting beside Lau Shen, began the first of many quiet conversations. Abbess Trishan tuned her internal rhythms to the primordial forces, augmenting her wisdom and prescient abilities. She sensed the latent power residing within Lau Shen and knew that the shattered woman was destined for greatness. She just needed a little guidance, and Abbess Trishan was the woman who could provide it.

"Months passed before the conversations came around to Lau Shen's life and the events that decimated her. Lau Shen had healed to the point that she was candid with Abbess Trishan. She related her life growing up at The Rose, and she was honest enough to include the cruelty and pain she caused others. Lau Shen wept as she recounted the eighty-one nights and Po's final dance of death and his gift of love to her. While she talked, Abbess Trishan quietly listened, nodding encouragement. For the first time, Lau Shen shared her pain.

"Upon hearing about the black dragon who had raised the tempest, the abbess speculated that an egg had washed down the river from the high mountains and lay dormant in the river until the time was right for hatching. She added, 'Dragons always rise fully formed with devastating storms and wind. We received word of black dragons fighting in the White Mountains north of here. Possibly related to the dragon from Leelan.' Lau Shen dully listened to the abbess's conjecture and remained quiet for the rest of the day.

"The years passed as Lau Shen settled into the Covenant life. She studied arduously, learning all she could about dragons and their nature and connection to the life forces. Meditation was a daily affair, and through it, her body, mind, and spirit became harmonized. Lau Shen began writing poems of the anxiety, loneliness, and pathos in love, but eventually, her poetry forced her to confront the truth that those negative emotions were hers because her love for Po was imperfect. Perfect love is only comprised of love, nothing else.

"Her beauty returned, but it was different from her youth. Gone was the vanity and arrogance, and in its place, an inner beauty formed of serenity and kindheartedness radiated outward into elegance. She was well-liked, her companions many, but there was a special bond she shared with Abbess Trishan. It was the deep friendship of confidants who shared their painful secrets, but it was also the intimate affinity between sage and prodigy.

"As more years elapsed, Lau Shen equaled the aged Abbess Trishan in wisdom and prophecy. One spring morning at daylight, an odd smell awakened Lau Shen. In the grayness a vision came. A skull lay in a murky field by a mountain lake. As she approached it, a wind from the lake blew through the skull's eye sockets, making a sound of desperate suffering. Stirring from the haunting vision, Lau Shen realized for the first time her purpose in life and immediately prepared to move on from the Covenant of Dragons.

"Nothing needed to be said to Abbess Trishan. She knew when she first attended to the pathetic woman years ago that she had a destiny to fulfill. Lau Shen came out of her grotto dressed in a clean khaki-colored robe of the order with a khaki satchel across her chest — khaki, as the color of the dust of the earth, symbolic to the Covenant for one's place in the universe. Abbess Trishan met her at the cave entrance and, after a prolonged hug, handed Lau Shen a walking stick carved as a black dragon rising, just like Madam Zu San's. The abbess had this carved many months ago in anticipation of this moment. With her black dragon staff. Lau Shen walked north out of the Dragon Grottoes, past the Dragon's Gate, and into the foothills of the White Mountains.

"Lau Shen followed the Golden River north toward its headwaters in the mist-covered, rugged, white peaks. It was a very different journey from the one years ago that took her to the Dragon Grottoes. In the villages nestled along the river she was welcomed, for her khaki clothing and demeanor told everyone that she was an itinerant sage on a pilgrimage. The black dragon walking staff implied that the pilgrimage was to Fire Dragon Mountain, the tallest volcanic peak of the White Mountains, the snow-covered volcanic mountain range famously inhabited by a fury of black dragons.

"The foothills she traveled were richly forested with pines, maples, and elms. Enormous, thick bull pines, standing alone like sentinels, towered above the hardwoods. The forests were rich with edible plants, berries, fruits, and nuts that fed a bear population. Small, reddish-brown deer were abundant, providing easy game for humans and for the leopards, wolves, and tigers. Because of the plenitude of deer, the tigers generally did not pose a threat to humans. Lau Shen saw tiger tracks during her journey, but using her abilities with the magical force, she created vibrational rhythms that repulsed the formidable beasts. This she learned at the Covenant, for there was something about tigers that was repugnant to dragons. Dragons did not like tigers and used their supernatural control to drive them away, and so did Lau Shen.

"Deep into the foothills, Lau Shen came upon the first of many tall cone stacks of stones. These were trail markers showing the way to Fire Dragon Mountain. Lau Shen saw them as artistic earthwork and delighted in each one. As she approached a summit, she could see over the treetops to the mountains encircling the solitary grandeur of Fire Dragon Mountain, but something was amiss. The light of the deep-blue sky was vivid on the Fire Dragon Mountain peak, yet a gloom surrounded the smaller mountains hugging its slopes. With resolve, Lau Shen tramped up the path through forests of mountain birch and pine to the town of Dragonhorn.

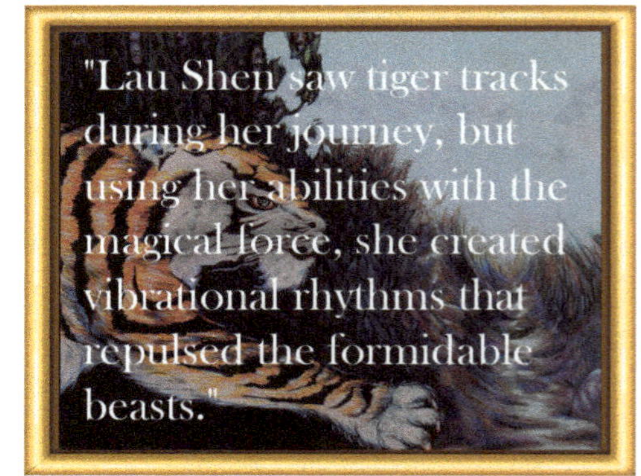

"Dragonhorn was situated on a spit of land thrust into the largest crater lake in the volcanic White Mountains. The town was atop a craggy bluff dotted with dwarf pines grabbing toeholds in the rock, trying not to tumble into the frigid water. Surrounding the town and the crater lake were lush, deep green forests, contrasted by copses of raku-like, white and black-barked birch. The crater lake of Dragonhorn was known as Big Dragon Lake, and at a saddle point in its rim south of the town, crystal-clear water flowed into a waterfall that joined waterfalls from the other lakes to make up the headwaters of the Golden River. Fire Dragon Mountain, towering above, was a steep-sloped volcano, whose deep, caldera lake produced the waterfall known as 'The Eternal Spring of Fire Dragon Mountain.'

"Dragonhorn was a holy site. Each crater lake harbored a black dragon, while other dragons inhabited lava caves, protecting the troves of gems, diamonds, gold, and minerals belched up from the earth's belly by the volcanoes. With dragon sightings becoming increasingly rare across the land, this fury of black dragons in the White Mountains attracted pilgrimages to Dragonhorn, which developed a reputation for piety as the town attended to the dragon devout.

"Coming into the rocky grass field on the town's outskirts, Lau Shen was startled to walk into a mist. Pulling out her shawl from the satchel, she masked her mouth and nose and entered Dragonhorn. The very fine particles suspended in the air obscured the sunlight, rendering the town in perpetual twilight. The streets were virtually deserted; the few people moving around were veiled as she was, and everyone had the haunted eyes of prolonged suffering. The steep A-frame buildings, the trees, everything was dusted over with an ashy residue that lent a sicky pallor to the whole town. Looking around, Lau Shen spied a carved relief of a dragon above the entrance to a stone building, which she assumed must be a sanctuary. Using the bronze, dragon-head knocker, she banged the heavy, wooden door and was greeted by a diminutive, balding man, who introduced himself as Brother Jac.

"The air inside the sanctuary was breathable, but despair emanated from the flickering shadows cast by the fireplace. Brother Jac, dressed in a black robe, lowered his eyes respectfully as he spoke to Lau Shen. 'I am of the Brotherhood of Black Dragons, who minister to the dragons of our mountains. I see by your robe that you come from the Covenant of Dragons.' He glanced down at her black dragon staff. 'Have you come to assist us in our dire situation?'

" 'Brother Jac, my name is Lau Shen, and I am indeed from the Covenant. I have been under the tutelage of Abbess Trishan for many years. I received a vision that spoke of death and desolation, and so I ventured north and arrived here just now. Perhaps if you tell me what has happened, I can see if there is something I can do to help.'

"Brother Jac led Lau Shen to a chair and, dusting off the film of ash, invited her to sit. 'It all started with a black dragon who flew in from the south many years ago.' Brother Jac, speaking in a measured and hushed tone, settled into describing the tragedy that befell Dragonhorn. When Lau Shen heard of the black dragon from the south, a chill shivered through her. Closing her eyes and slowing her breathing, she controlled her internal rhythms and allowed the words of Brother Jac to flow into her.

"Dragonhorn and the White Mountains had been in peace for generations. With the fury of black dragons settled into their respective territories, the town was blessed with nourishing rainfall and a bountiful life. The dragon of the town, Kiu Lung, spent her time in the depths of Big Dragon Lake or in a volcanic cave on the plateau just above the town. The Brotherhood attended her, and all was well. That was, until the dragon from the south arrived seeking his own territory. Dragon battles ensued all over the White Mountains with tremendous storms, lightning, and wind, until the upstart dragon finally challenged Kiu Lung of Dragonhorn, a female dragon of great age.

"The battle was ferocious, and the destruction widespread. Several days they fought in the lake, in the air above the town, and down into the volcanic caves. The lake was befouled and crested a tidal wave that washed over the town. Tempests of tornadoes and thunderstorms demolished buildings, and disrupted lava oozed out of the vents of Fire Dragon Mountain, setting the forest on fire. The combat did not cease at night as both dragons vomited lightning down upon the town, transforming the darkness into a staccato of light. As the fight raged on, the townspeople became desperate, and they turned to the Brotherhood for help.

"The Brotherhood was severely pressured by their neighbors, but they well knew the old admonishment: 'When dragons fight, they are not looking at us, so we should not look at them; if we do not seek the ferocity of the dragons, they also will not seek us.' The battle would continue until the issue of territory was decided, and humans should not get involved; this the Brothers understood. Eventually, the wailing of the people was so great, they relented and made clay likenesses of the dragons, and gathered bones and filth to make a foul smudge. When the fighting peaked overhead, the Brothers burned the smudge, sending the nasty smoke up to the battling dragons, while the people screamed at the images, flogging the clay dragons to make them stop.

"At that same moment, Kiu Lung had twisted back into a position to make a lethal strike on the younger dragon, when she was distracted by the hullabaloo below, which allowed the upstart dragon to clamp down on her tail, severing a portion of it. Kiu Lung roared a thunder that flattened everyone to the ground. In her rage, she spiraled down from her opponent, then quickly darting up, she seized him by the underside of his neck, viciously shook it until it snapped, and threw his broken body into a flaming flow of lava below. The Brothers regained their feet and looked up together to see the unspeakable terror of Kiu Lung glancing backward at them with eyes gleaming with fire, as she flew into her cave.

"Upon hearing about the demise of the black dragon who caused Po Agg's death, Lau Shen pondered her feelings and decided she felt nothing. Nothing, except love for Po, a love embedded forever. Lau Shen asked, 'What happened to cause this suffocating mist?'

"Brother Jac kept his face averted and admitted, 'We, the Brotherhood, made a mistake and intruded where we should not have. Kiu Lung was very angry and caused this to punish us. She never comes out of her cave, just the mist from time to time. Nothing we do to make amends has any effect, so we suffer and endure. Many neighbors have left, but for most of us, this is home. One does not easily walk away from home.'

"Not unless one's heart is torn asunder and love is gone, Lau Shen thought fleetingly; then she turned her attention back to Dragonhorn. Dragons, she knew, have the power to produce fire and water from their mouths, and they have supernatural control of earth and air as well. In her lava cave, Kiu Lung used her blue fire and heated volcanic rock to a glowing, molten mass. Then producing water and using vibrational control of the air to generate tremendous pressure, she blasted the molten rock out into the cold, mountain air, spewing it forth as extremely minute crystalized particles that suspended in the air. Lau Shen had an idea of what to do, and it required her to dance once again after so many years.

"My life comes full circle, she mused. No, no, not a circle; that's not right. A spiral. My life spirals, and once again I dance, but this time I bring years of pain and suffering, and years of friendship and love — all that I experienced and learned, all that I was, and all that I am now, will enflame my dancing, but not vanity. No! Now, I dance with love!

"That was the power behind Po Agg's dancing — how he touched her heart. At that instant, Lau Shen's mind was enlightened into clarity. The spiral of life rotates on the harmony of body, mind, and spirit, continuously revolving inward toward the singularity of perfect love. Lau Shen trembled as the potency of the spiritual force rushed in and infused her with compassion. She was ready to dance to save Dragonhorn and its people.

"Brother Jac watched Lau Shen silently, and slowly backed away, astonished, as the air around her crackled and her body began to glow. Lau Shen looked over at him and crinkled a questioning brow at the peculiar expression on his face. 'Please take me to the cave of Kiu

Lung,' she requested. Brother Jac remained silent, bowed his willingness, and made a motion to the other Brothers, standing awestruck at the back of the sanctuary. Together in the evening light, they paraded into the mist and up the path to the abode of the black dragon.

"As the group approached the cave on Fire Dragon Mountain, the Brothers were puzzled when Lau Shen asked them to sing along with whatever sound they might hear as she danced. Sing, dance? Looking oddly at each other, they agreed to do so. They walked on a little further together, until the Brothers stayed in a wooded area, discretion overcoming their curiosity. Lau Shen continued to the flat, grassy ground in front of the cave. Rocks and boulders were strewn here and there, the grass thick and matted. Brother Jac shook his head in confusion as Lau Shen, after tying up her robe to free her legs, stood in front of the cave for a long time in a stilled pose, arms outstretched as if hugging a tree. His confusion changed to wonderment, as the mist-filled air crackled around her, and she began to glow.

"Finally, the sage, famous as Lau Shen for the mystery and magic of her dance, began to move, tentatively at first, but then more assertively as her body and mind woke to the memory of who she was, what she was. She was Lau Shen, the greatest dancer of all time, who now danced and leaped, turned and spiraled over the grass, upon the boulders, and into the air with the pure love of Po in her heart, moving with an energy and intensity never equaled. All the primordial forces forged themselves within her being, merging her with the universe's spiritual force. The air began to hum, echoing off the slopes of the surrounding White Mountains. The Brothers, their skin and hair tingling with the electricity crackling around them, raised their voices in echo-heightened harmony and sang as a holy choir, reverberating the song of dance through the mountains and across the dragon lakes.

"Lau Shen danced on, powerfully, elegantly, with creativity and magic manifesting themselves in her every movement, their rhythms affecting everything. At the apogee of her dance of love, Lau Shen pirouetted, faster and faster, the air spinning with her into a whirlwind, as the crystalline mist over Dragonhorn sparkled like minute diamonds. On and on, Lau Shen pirouetted, beyond human endurance, until the air throughout the White Mountains and upon the peak of Fire Dragon Mountain radiated with the brilliant glow of an aurora. Red and blue curtains of ionized light spiraled into a miraculous spectacle.

"The Brothers never stopped singing. They were too terrified to stop, for out of her cave strode Kiu Lung, attracted by the phenomena, as were the black dragons from the whole of the White Mountains, hovering above the aurora's brightness. They all stared at the spinning woman as Lau Shen gradually slowed down and finally collapsed on the grass, still radiating the spiritual force. Lau Shen sat back on her knees and, facing Kiu Lung, she offered a deep bow of respect to the bob-tailed dragon, her forehead touching the matted grass. Lau Shen then turned to the group of dragons watching from above and offered the same gesture of homage.

"Kiu Lung, curiosity flickering across her eyes, nodded acceptance of the adulation, and raised her regal face toward her fellow dragons to roar out a sustained, jingling-jangling, melodious roar. The fury of black dragons above mimicked her. The Brothers harmonized with the dragons, still too petrified to stop singing. The red and blue aurora fluctuated with the rhythm of the dragons' roaring and shifted into glittering, intense pink arcs. Each arc flashed from dragon to dragon until every dragon was sparkling in pink luminescence, pulsing in sequence to the night sky's pink aurora. Kiu Lung and the entire fury of dragons gaped at each other in wonder and delight.

"The dragons in their pleasure issued forth from their mouths gentle rains that poured down to wash away the smothering gloom, as a blessing to the town. The calamitous mist that had grieved the town for so long was no more. Lau Shen had saved Dragonhorn.

"Kiu Lung strutted over to Lau Shen, while the other black dragons watched from above. Lau Shen glanced up into the dragon's eyes, then quickly averted her eyes. A long moment of silence hung in the air. Lau Shen was still vibrating with the spiritual rhythm. She could feel it. So could Kiu Lung. 'You may look me in the eyes, if you wish, for you are protected,' voiced the coppery tones of the dragon as her bobbed tail swished around to carefully enclose the glowing dancer. Lau Shen looked up into the intensity and fire of the dragon's eyes and was jolted by an unexpected rhythm that synchronized with hers. Lau Shen watched as Kiu Lung studied her, felt the dragon exploring her rhythms and divining her essence. In her metallic, lyrical voice, Kiu Lung asked, 'What is your name, child?' Lau Shen answered, and the dragon continued, 'Lau Shen, I would like you to return to me here in nine full moons.' Looking over at the Brothers gathered in a tight group, she added, 'And bring Brother Jac with you.' Lau Shen lowered her eyes. 'As you say, and thank you.'

"Kiu Lung strode back into her cave, while the black dragons flew back to their lairs. Lau Shen stood up and, adjusting her robe, staggered to the Brothers, who had finally stopped singing to watch the unheard-of interaction between the dancer and the dragon. Nothing was said as they descended in the night to the sanctuary. The next morning the town of Dragonhorn woke to the glory of deep-blue sky and sun, the first mist-free morning in many years. Everyone rejoiced and then offered their reverent thanks when the Brothers told them of Lau Shen, the sage and dancer, who made the magic to appease their dragon, Kiu Lung, finally.

"Nine moons passed quickly for Lau Shen. It was a time for meditation and connection with her new surroundings. Her dance on Fire Dragon Mountain had changed her. The dramatic infusion of the spiritual force with her rhythms put her in touch with life around her. She felt the living nature of the rocks, lakes, mountains — all of nature. The music of the entire universe that set the stars, seas, and winds in motion rejoiced within her to an ecstatic crescendo.

"In her enlightened state, Lau Shen's knowledge of the perfect rhythms embodied in the life forces allowed her to recognize unnatural movements and broken rhythms in the thoughts and actions of others, and to perceive when the symmetry and balance of the life rhythms were out of whack. These abilities gave her a heightened gift of prophecy, for she could comprehend where a course of action would lead given the nature of its rhythm, and with that understanding could ascertain what was necessary to put the rhythm in proper balance. Lau Shen was sought throughout Dragonhorn for her spiritual guidance. By the end of the nine months, she was lauded by all as the sage and prophetess of the White Mountains.

"On the designated evening, the moon peered around the volcano's steep slope, as Lau Shen and Brother Jac hiked up the trail to the cave of Kiu Lung. Lau Shen was at peace; Brother Jac was apprehensive, as he did not know why his presence was demanded. The possible reasons for it gave him pause, having no idea if maybe he was walking to his doom. Fear struck deeply into his heart, when they reached the cave entrance, to see the entire fury of black dragons from the White Mountains assembled around the waiting Kiu Lung. Lau Shen dropped to her knees in front of the entourage and offered again her deep bow, while poor, trembling Brother Jac already was prostrated on the grass. Kiu Lung looked at Brother Jac with an amused expression, and motioned them to stand,

"Lau Shen stood relaxed before the regal dragons. Brother Jac was hunched in his robe like a turtle hiding in his shell. Kiu Lung spoke in a soft, pleasant voice, in sharp contrast to the fierce, dragon visage she presented. 'Lau Shen, I speak for the fury of black dragons of the White Mountains. We bestow on you the title of the Dragon Mother. You now have a special relationship with us. As such, you have the freedom to seek us out as you wish. You are the intermediary in our dealings with people of these mountains. We will communicate to them through you, and you will act on their behalf before us. Do you, Lau Shen, accept this charge?'

"Lau kept her face solemn, but inside she was beaming with happiness. 'I do, thank you.'

" 'Brother Jac, you are here to witness this charge bestowed upon Lau Shen, and to acknowledge to the other Brothers and the people in Dragonhorn that Lau Shen is to be known henceforth as the Dragon Mother. She will be called that, and she will be treated with the same respect as we expect toward us. In addition, the Brotherhood is to serve and assist her in whatever she might need. Do this, and Dragonhorn and the people of the White Mountains will receive our blessings. Do you understand?'

"Brother Jac stood a little taller as he answered, 'Yes, my Dragon.' He gave her a small bow of respect.

"Kiu Lung, turning her attention back to Lau Shen, said quietly, 'Walk with me, Dragon Mother.' Lau Shen and the imposing, bob-tailed dragon moved away from the other dragons and out of Brother Jac's earshot. 'What I tell you now is vital for your progression toward complete, spiritual integration. You have come far in developing your internal rhythms of creativity and magic; rhythms that can birth new possibilities of reality. Your dance for the Dragonhorn people was rich with the powers of these two rhythms, but more importantly, the dance was infused with the rhythm of love. This attracted the spiritual rhythm of the universe to resonate with your inner rhythms, taking them to levels of enormous power. Recognize, sense, feel, and know this integration of the rhythms. Meditate, nourish, and enhance your alliance to the forces of the universe. Become one with them. Cultivate an absolute affinity for the spiritual force, and when the time is right, I will call you, and you will come to me. Together, I will assist you in the transformation.'

" 'I will do as you say, but I do not understand. What transformation?'

" 'The transformation into dragonhood, Lau Shen.' "

Li-Dan, in the guise of his former self, Lao Tzu, stretched out his arms and yawned. I was trembling, a combination of the chill and an emotional reaction to the Dragon Mother's story. I sat still for a long time; as did Li-Dan, anticipating the customary questions from me.

"Li-Dan, why did you tell me this story?" I finally asked.

"Because the Dragon Mother asked me to tell you," he answered nonchalantly.

"And why did the Dragon Mother want you to do that?"

"David, that is a question to ask the Dragon Mother, but did you not appreciate how the story concluded? Dragonhood! That should be your foremost question."

In a weak attempt to defend myself, I responded, "Well, Li-Dan, that was my next question. I was just so intrigued by the Dragon Mother's life that I was distracted."

Li-Dan flashed a knowing smirk. "Distracted? She bewitched you, as she did Po?"

"No, I was bewitched by who she became when love entered her heart. How could I not be? Tell me, Li-Dan, about her transformation into dragonhood."

Li-Dan stood up and tottered around a bit to stretch his scrawny legs, before plopping down again to continue.

"The Dragon Mother served the White Mountains well for many years. Pilgrims regularly sojourned to Dragonhorn, so her reputation spread far and wide throughout the lands. Eventually, people traveled specifically to consult with the Dragon Mother, and she helped all. The more people from different lands and cultures that she helped, the more love and compassion she felt for all humankind. That love grew within her until it manifested in her every thought and action and radiated out to inspire those around her to see the unity and beauty of all life in the world.

"Her meditations were deeper, richer, and allowed her control of her inner rhythms and the synchronizations with the cosmic forces. She visited the In-Between and grew in spiritual strength until the day she sensed the calling from Kiu Lung. At that moment, the Dragon Mother was three days' journey through the White Mountains from the bob-tailed dragon's cave, but she immediately heeded the summons. As she approached the cave entrance, Kiu Lung perceived her approach and was waiting for her. 'You are ready, Lau Shen. Please climb upon my back, and I will assist you in your final transformation into dragonhood.' Lau Shen, the Dragon Mother, did as she was instructed and rose up with the bob-tailed, black dragon into the dark, stormy clouds forming high above the peak of Fire Dragon Mountain.

"Brother Jac, peering up into the tumultuous cloud mass from the courtyard of the sanctuary, caught sight of Kiu Lung with the Dragon Mother perched atop her massive, serpentine shape as they spiraled up into the dense mist and disappeared. From deep within the clouds, lights flashed, illuminating the town below, as vibrational waves rippled down, engulfing Dragonhorn. Brother Jac's small body tingled in harmony with the pulsing and, overcome with happiness, he lifted his face and laughed with unrestrained joy as the deep-blue sky once again glowed overhead. The Dragon Mother and Kiu Lung were gone and were never seen again in the White Mountains."

Yellow Dragon in Waterfall

11
Spiritual Dragons

Rainer Maria Rilke

hat does one say to an ending like that — ascension to dragonhood! Li-Dan knew what to say: "The dragon's bounty is as profound as the ocean, and the Dragon Mother's virtue is as lofty as the hills." It sounded like a venerated aphorism from a distant past.

I stared for some time at the ocean as dawn revealed waves whipping up foam, driven by an assertive northeaster. "So, Li-Dan, what is meant by dragonhood?" I asked as I turned back to him. Li-Dan, as Lao Tzu, was not there. I looked around and spotted a small snake, banded with five colors, slithering toward the wild brush behind the dunes. It stopped and, gathering its length in a coil, raised its head.

"The Dragon Mother will come to you soon. Be patient, for she will answer your questions, and stop gongoozling me, David," he hissed. Then, flittering his little forked tongue, he gave me a snaky smile.

"How does he do that?" I muttered as Li-Dan the snake slid away behind the dunes and into a tangle of palmettos.

Gazing at the sun rising out of the watery horizon, I flashed upon a memory of the salutations that I offered with my newly born sons. Perched at the edge of the primary dunes, I introduced my boys to the earth's sand, and to the charged, ocean breezes laden with the salt smell, and to the ocean as the source of life. The final salutation was to the emerging sun, in its rising glory showing the promise of renewal — as did my sons, life's promise for starting anew.

I would have offered salutations to the dragons, as embodiments of these primal elements and forces of nature, but the rituals happened before I met the Dragon Mother and Li-Dan and they revealed the existence of dragons. Still, instinctively I was compelled — by what? — the creative force within me, maybe, to begin my sons' lives in harmony with the world's living energies. I suppose that it was to the dragons that I offered greetings on my sons' behalf; I just did not realize it at the time.

The wind was blowing briskly off the ocean. Barefooted, I ran down the beach, pushed along by the strong gusts at my back until I reached the beach cottage. Invigorated from the wind-augmented run that turned me into a racer, I was no longer tired or sleepy. Nevertheless, after the night with Li-Dan, I believed contemplation was in order. Assuming a standing pose and facing south, I lifted my arms in front and, holding them there, I relaxed into a soft breathing rhythm, allowing unimpeded thoughts to flow. Almost immediately, I felt a familiar presence and joy rippled through me.

"Good morning, David. I will come to you the next full moon and we will talk."

Through my smile I whispered, "I look forward to it, Dragon Mother."

It was a good month. I was as happy as I could be. I could not help the excitement trembling in me at the prospect of seeing her again. I tried to understand my euphoria over the Dragon Mother. Certainly, part of it was intrigue with the mysticism that revolved around her, the In-Between, and dragonhood, but it was more than the transcendental nature inherent in these. I was captivated by who she was, by the woman Lau Shen. My interactions with her provided insight into her essence, which was loving and brilliant. I was smitten with the Dragon Mother. Laughing, I asked myself, "Is it preposterous to have profound feelings for someone thirty-thousand odd years older than me?"

Dark gray clouds hung low overhead on the day of the full moon, mimicking twilight by early afternoon. Strong breezes whipped the drizzly rain, but I decided to walk along the beach anyway before my evening rendezvous. A drab day and turbulent showers did not diminish my exuberance; soon I would see the Dragon Mother again. With bared feet kicking up the drifting piles of sea foam, I strolled along the surf fringe north toward the turtle dune. The weather had driven everyone indoors but me, so I was alone with my thoughts. Water dripped off my matted hair, trickling to the tip of my nose, to hang there before plopping down to my shirt. I ignored the drops, for in my mind's eye I was engrossed in recalling her splendid form. Grace, elegance, and beauty in her every movement — in her every action and word. The Dragon Mother was exquisite and refined.

A thunderous roar jolted me out of my pleasant musings. Instinctively, I dropped into a tense crouch, body trembling and heart racing, not sure if I needed to fight or run. Frantically, as I scoured the area, golden movement flashed from a pitch-black cloud seething overhead. A metallic screech rippled through clouds, throwing me to my knees. I knew what it was. The knowing did not stop the horror that grabbed me and closed my throat as I looked up into the terrifying, fiery eyes and grimacing mouth of a ferocious golden dragon, so monstrously huge I could not see the end of her. The Dragon Mother had arrived.

The Dragon Mother in her dragon form gradually reduced her size as she descended to the sandy beach. Poised majestically before me, she was smaller, yes, but still she towered over my puny, quivering body. Her open maw pulsed as she breathed in and out, blue fire flickering with each breath. Her fiery eyes overwhelmed me. I was afraid to move, much less speak, and all thoughts of the elegant and refined woman had fled my mind. Deep within her dragon's throat a clanging rumble made its way to her gaping mouth, as if she was clearing her throat to speak to me. Or perhaps to blast me with dragon fire. I gasped a breath and froze.

"Hi, David! Surprised to see me?" sounded out the Dragon Mother's rich, melodious voice.

"Dragon Mother! You scared the hell out of me!" I blurted, my eyes tearing with relief.

"Oh, David. It was not my intention to frighten you, but only to help you understand something very important. Here, just a minute." The air around the golden-yellow dragon shimmered, increasing in intensity as the dragon shape blurred until it was gone and standing calmly before me was the Dragon Mother in her exquisite beauty.

"Are you more comfortable now?" she said, her voice laced with kindness and concern.

Feeling a little ashamed, I lowered my head and nodded, "Yes, thank you."

Tenderly, she took my hand and led me to the turtle dune. Glancing sideways at me with an impish grin, she tilted her head to the clouds above. I felt a subtle vibration resonating from her, and looking up myself, I was startled to see the rain clouds dissipate until the late afternoon sun shone brightly down. Then, lowering her face to the soaked sand under us, she opened her mouth wide and huffed out warmed breath until the sand was dry enough for us to sit.

"Okay, that was a little strange," I mumbled.

The Dragon Mother beamed at me, laughed, and warmed me to my core. Getting comfortable upon the sand, she began. "You needed to see me in dragon form to fully comprehend that I am a dragon. I am also Lau Shen, but Lau Shen transformed into a spiritual dragon. I know Li-Dan has spoken of this, but words and the smack of reality do not have the same effect. You remember that there are three kinds of dragons, yes?"

I nodded that I did. "Li-Dan explained the earthly dragons and the celestial dragons — or rather, the Celestial Dragon of Destruction. He told me that you wanted to talk with me about the spiritual dragons."

"Yes, I want to discuss spiritual dragons with you personally, David, but I asked Li-Dan to relate my story to you, so you might have a more personal understanding of dragonhood. The three kinds of dragons are related, although the Celestial Dragon of Destruction, forming out of the universe's vast energy, is special. Its power is beyond comprehension and it is called into being solely for ending an Age. Earthly dragons and spiritual dragons are very much alike, but with different sources and for different purposes. Spiritual dragons have the same form and general nature as earthly dragons. We have the same supernatural powers; thus, we exercise similar influences over the elements and the primordial forces. We are of this earth, but not as the earthly dragons are. Spiritual dragons come from the sons and daughters of the earth, people born of the earth, who are raised into dragonhood." She paused to let her words implant deeply within me.

"You must have a sense of this from your conversations with Li-Dan." I did have a sense of it. This was the crux of "The Pink Dragons of the Aurora," the Dragon Mother's story.

The Dragon Mother continued, "By successfully developing the internal rhythms of magic, creativity, and love to the point that they resonate harmoniously with the primordial rhythms, one comes into synchronization with the spiritual rhythm, resulting in the ultimate expression of the vital spirit with the rhythm of life. The vital spirit is the sum of the rhythms each person possesses, including the rhythms of thought, emotion, and intention. All life has a vital spirit, including dragons. To elevate into dragonhood, the vital spirit of a person must attain a certain level of energization, with the desire and intention to reach dragonhood."

I must have looked confused because the Dragon Mother stopped her discussion and studied me. I looked at her long, sloped eyelids lying over shimmering golden eyes, and I sighed.

"What's the matter, David?" she whispered in her rich, alluring voice, and I sighed again.

"Dragon Mother, why a transformation into a dragon?" I asked.

The full moon shone low in the night sky, its mellow glow enhancing the delicate golden aura adorning the Dragon Mother. Her eyes were transfixed upon my face, which both delighted and unnerved me. When I averted my eyes, gently she spoke again. "The answer to that question is found in the origin and nature of dragons. Dragons have supernatural control of the primordial forces and the prime elements; thus, all life is under their influence. All three kinds of dragons do this, but with each to their own purpose.

"The spiritual dragons, who are people raised to dragonhood, interact directly with individuals, helping them to free their minds and obtain happiness. Spiritual dragons touch the subconscious of those people who seek understanding about life and the nature of the world. Spiritual dragons are attracted to those individuals who seek freedom of mind and spirit, and to people who equate the life of humankind with the life of nature. Spiritual dragons especially touch the lives of sages, for sages have a deep compassion and comprehension of the struggles with the dual nature that all humankind encounters — depression, joy, frustration, success, suffering, triumph, degradation, respect, loneliness, and love.

"Spiritual dragons prepare the sages to pass their insights on to others; the sages are people who are given to thought and meditation, seeking through self-cultivation the wisdom of the infinite, and who through their understanding of the dragons' way solicit the dragons' blessings for their community. Their understanding and wisdom are based on experiences with people and with the natural order of life, both of which guide their development and their striving for harmony and balance. This necessitates that sages have a life rich with varied experiences."

The Dragon Mother stopped talking and looked out over the water at the moon's reflection. Her faraway look told me she was recalling a distant memory, so I said nothing and waited. With a slight headshake, she continued. "Creative people and those strongly attuned to the magic and love inherent in the cosmos, like the sages, are enhanced by the primordial forces and instinctively seek enlightenment. By seeking enlightenment, they are pursuing the dragons. 'Dragons live in the pure water of wisdom and dance in the clear water of life.' "

Ah, another ancient aphorism, I thought. "And how does that result in transformation into dragonhood?" I asked, trying to get a clearer grasp on this fantastic notion.

"By being in total synchronization with the forces, one feels the same supernatural powers inherent in the dragons. One begins to understand what it means to be a dragon, to be in harmony with the forces of the universe and to have control of the primal elements of our world. It is a realization of the oneness of all existence, and an inner awareness of being complete and whole. This is the exhilarating feeling of freedom and bliss. This is enlightenment.

"A person can only get so far toward total enlightenment on their own. For transformation into dragonhood, it takes the assistance of a dragon, earthly or spiritual, to complete the final integration of someone with the spiritual force. This final integration cannot happen without a completely committed intention to reach the level of dragonhood."

The Dragon Mother drifted up, and standing before me, she offered her hand to help me to my feet. I fully realized her nature in her handclasp — enormous strength and power wrapped in the velvet softness of her touch. "David, walk with me."

We strolled north along the high tide mark until we reached the jetties, two runs of granite boulders out into the surf on either side of the river channel as it emptied into the ocean. The Dragon Mother motioned for me to sit beside her on a flat rock at the water's edge. Large, cockroach-like critters, surprised by our presence, scurried into crevices. A river rat shadowed by the moonlight watched us for a few moments before nonchalantly resuming its search for food. The Dragon Mother took no notice of these creatures. I found them creepy.

After a few moments of silence, the Dragon Mother spoke. "The love that Po offered me awakened the rhythm of love lying dormant within me — stirred it so that the primordial rhythm of love was able to touch this nascent rhythm. Mothers' love for their newly born babies is the love that awakens the internal rhythms of love in their children. Fathers' love nourishes the rhythm, but without this initial awakening, the awareness and development of love's internal rhythm is damaged. Life's tribulations can further inhibit the ability to know love. The rampant influences of ego, desire, and fear make love impossible."

"But what is love, Dragon Mother?" I asked.

A small movement caught my eye. One of those creepy-crawly bugs was scampering over the Dragon Mother's leg. I shivered with the urge to swipe it away. The Dragon Mother serenely gathered the creature in her hand and tenderly placed it safely in a crevice. With that small gesture, she taught me what I needed to understand. We looked at each other and she said, "Reverence for all life, David. That is the essence of love."

Li-Dan as the Old Master

12

Azure Dragon Rising

Rainer Maria Rilke

he Dragon Mother and I sat there watching the waves rolling in to meet the river rushing out, the mingled water slapping the jetties in cadence. It was peaceful sitting together on the boulders and watching the lighthouse cast its revolving beacon upon the ocean. I was startled when the Dragon Mother spoke softly, "The painter becomes what he paints."

That snapped me to attention. At last, an explanation for that cryptic message jingling in my head months ago.

"By now, David, you should have a sense of what that means. To have profound respect and connection with the entire creation frees the mind to know perfect love. To accomplish this, you must overcome the inner demons of ego, desire, and fear. To overcome these demons, it is imperative to go within and release them. Meditation is critical for this, but there are other pathways. For you, one is clear — painting.

"The creative process is one of loneliness and, like meditation, delves inward in pursuit of illumination and truth. Activating and developing your creativity naturally attracts the primordial force of creativity. As the creative force builds, your creativity draws the magical force to it, and ultimately the primordial force of love leads you to clarity for the beauty of the world. The spiritual force now resonates with your internal rhythms, providing divine guidance in your spiritual growth. You become attuned to the rhythmical movement of life in the world — your paintings and you radiate that life and become as one — 'the painter becomes what he paints.' "

A squall gusted off the ocean, blowing hair across my eyes. Shaking my face into the wind to clear my sight, I looked out upon the dark expanse of the water. The waves, agitated with whitecaps, smacked the jetties with increasing fury. Even after years of living by the ocean, a touch of fear quivered in me when it showed its ferocity; the fear recalling childhood memories of vulnerability, lying on the bed at night, wide-eyed and trembling into the vast darkness.

Among the Dragon Mother's remarkable abilities, she was foremost a seer divining truths, so I was not surprised when she asked me, "Do you fear death, David?"

"Reading my mind, Dragon Mother?" I said.

She sat serenely with an expression that said, "Silly boy, that's not so hard."

After a moment's reflection, I answered, "Perhaps not fear of death as much as fear of the unknown."

"David, death is not an unknown," she casually remarked. "At death the body's vital energy disperses out into the cosmos, ultimately, a part of the spiritual force from which it came. The material body that remains is absorbed into life's movement."

The pearl on the chain around her neck began to glow golden as the Dragon Mother's hand elegantly traced a spiral into the windstorm. Immediately, calm surrounded the jetties as a pleasant breeze rippled over the waves. All anxiety left me as I realized I was safe in the Dragon Mother's presence.

The Dragon Mother continued. "If the spiritual force resonates strongly within you, then at death something special happens. Its presence focuses and binds your vital energy, holding your internal rhythms intact for a time. If those rhythms are aligned to dragonhood, then dragons rise to offer transformation.

"What is offered is not immortality, for immortality is not possible, nor is it suited to life in the duality. It is a transformation into a higher life-form — the dragon, the divine embodiment manifesting the powers of life."

"So, Dragon Mother, transformation to dragonhood takes place at death?" I asked.

"Yes, it can, but transformation is possible anytime a person is radiant with the rhythm of the spiritual force, and there is an unwavering desire to be transformed. Spiritual dragons perceive a person's vital rhythms. They can enhance vital rhythms, or diminish them, and because the spiritual rhythm is integral to the dragons' nature, they are divinely guided to make the correct judgment — always.

"This is not what you expected to hear about dragons, is it?" the Dragon Mother asked.

"No, no it's not. The common notion of dragons is more like Li-Dan's terrifying description of the Celestial Dragon of Destruction," I admitted.

"Oh, David. Understand, the Celestial Dragon is real, and it is coming. This Age is approaching its end. The earthly dragons are dormant in preparation for the return. We spiritual dragons in the In-Between are very active helping those individuals receptive to the spiritual rhythm find their freedom."

The Dragon Mother paused and studied me for a few moments. She appeared to be measuring her words.

"Have you wondered why I have taken a personal interest in you? Why I sent Li-Dan to instruct you, and why I have come to you now?"

I choked, anticipating what the Dragon Mother, ever mystical and enchanting, might say. "I ... I asked Li-Dan that question, and he said that it was for you to answer."

"Indeed, it is. Remember in Lau Shen's story, Po elevated his creativity to such a level that the rhythms of magic infused him, and his love awakened love's rhythm within me. The purity of this love followed by his death destroyed the person who was Lau Shen. Out of destruction comes creativity with the ability to forge a new essence. The person I was did not understand the vital rhythm of Po. The dragon who I became can fathom his rhythms of love and creativity, and understand the magic he worked on me. As the Dragon Mother, I understand the vital rhythm that was Po.

"You see, David, without primordial love resonating in a person, pure love is impossible, for it becomes tainted by needs and desires. Satisfying mutual needs can sustain a relationship, perhaps, but not infuse a blissful love that seeks nothing, asks nothing, and gives all."

The Dragon Mother lowered her eyes for a moment and then, raising them to mine, breathed out, "Your vital rhythm recalls vividly the vital rhythm of Po. I feel a special connection with you, and this deepens my desire to help you find your way to dragonhood."

"Oh!" That was all that I could utter for a few moments. Then a thought came to me. "Dragon Mother, if you feel a connection with me, would my vital rhythm conversely feel a connection to you?" I added quietly, "Because, I have ... have felt a strange attraction to you that I cannot explain."

"Yes, David, the connection is mutual. Through all the Ages, people often sensed enigmatic connections with others. Everyone vibrates to a set of rhythms. The vital rhythm defines the individual, and it can be chaotic to harmonic. Negative and destructive thoughts, actions, or intentions disrupt the quality of the vital rhythm, as does a disconnect with the spiritual rhythm of life. These imbue a person with a life of dissonance — harsh and conflicting. To the extent that the vital rhythm is wholesome and in harmony with the rhythms of the creation, a person enjoys a life rich and full.

"An interconnection occurs between two people when their vital rhythms are alike. When the vital rhythms match, they resonate strongly with each other. The vital rhythm of one activates the other without any conscious intention.

"That was the connection Po and I had, even though I did not realize it at the time. It is the same connection that you and I have, David." The Dragon Mother looked at me, her intense dragon eyes softened by the serenity of her golden-hued face.

"This has nothing to do with the notion of reincarnation," she continued. "Po is Po, and you are you, but your vital rhythms are uncannily similar."

I was stunned into silence; my breathing went shallow and rapid. Instinctively, I sought the breath control of my meditations, and finding it, I slowly relaxed my mind and body until I could think again.

"But I do not possess the purity of his love. My ability to love is imperfect," I confessed.

"So was Po's originally; his desire and passion fueled his feelings for me. As his creativity increased over the eighty-one days, his obsession to create fantastic dance expressions to inflame my heart filled him with the cosmic creative rhythm. The magical rhythm then enchanted his dances with power and possibility, until finally, his dancing was infused with the purity of love.

"Do not underestimate the affinity that the primordial rhythms have for each other, David.

When I decided out of heartfelt concern to help the Dragonhorn people, I used the creativity of my dancing. As I danced, pure love filled my heart and magic bewitched my movements. Pirouetting beyond human endurance, I made the impossible become possible, and the pink aurora glowed and dazzled the black dragons. Our intense individual, creative rhythms attracted the spiritual rhythm to Po and me. That potential, David, exists within you. Your creativity can bring the spiritual rhythm powerfully into your life.

"Your vital rhythm must be harmonic, so be diligent with your meditations. The connection you and I share will be beneficial in your endeavors, and I will be a part of your spiritual journey. As you paint, consider this: 'The universe is revealed in the sacredness of the small and insignificant, and in the intervals, pauses, and quiet moments of active doing.' This will guide you in seeing the connection of the spiritual with the material and will endow your paintings with power."

The Dragon Mother stood up and faced the darkness of the ocean. "David, hold my arm, please."

Moving closely beside her, I gingerly embraced her arm. The calm bubble that shielded us from the storm disappeared, and the wind off the ocean whooshed in, twisting upward. To my alarm, we began to rise above the turbulent clouds. I had to remind myself that I was safe in the Dragon Mother's presence.

Again, she anticipated my thoughts. "Don't be apprehensive, David. I am taking you to the In-Between."

"The In-Between! How is that possible?" I hollered over the rush of wind. "I am not ready for the transformation!"

"This is not the transformation. This is a visit," said the Dragon Mother, her melodious voice cutting cleanly through the din.

"And it is possible," she chimed, "because I can control the magical rhythm — the impossible becomes possible, remember? I want you to experience the In-Between personally. It will assist your growth, and besides, would you not enjoy seeing Li-Dan again?"

Increasingly powerful vibrations battered me. My body started shaking vigorously, but I eked out, "I wo ... wo ... would." Alarm bells blared in my head as my vision blurred. The darkness of the night shimmered white before my mind slipped into nothingness.

With arms flailing, my mind flashed back into consciousness. Anxiously jerking my eyes open, I looked up into the amused face of the Dragon Mother. Sprawled on a grassy knoll, my head was cradled in her lap.

The Dragon Mother laughed as she said, "I'm sorry. I should have warned you. The transition into the In-Between is intense for those not dragons."

My mind was reeling in confusion as I stared up at the Dragon Mother. I was content to snuggle in her arms, but the brightness and clarity of the light stirred me to sit up and look around. I was amazed. The In-Between in person was far different from the In-Between of my meditations. It was still a Chinese landscape painting, but substantial — more of a physical place, less dreamlike. We were on a plateau that overlooked cloud-filled valleys that snaked through distant mists into jutting mountain peaks of multi-hued rocks and blue-green spruces. Thickets of red and orange azalea bloomed on the plateau, pierced by rocky outcrops and twisted pines. Waterfalls cascaded off the mountainsides, their tumbling chanting into the atmosphere.

There were dragons in their assorted colors everywhere across the lush terrain, the brilliance of the mountain light wrapping them in auras. Across the ravine, a male yellow dragon, his tongue flailing and bellowing gonging thunder, burst through a waterfall. I sat there for a long time gawking at the wonder of it all until the Dragon Mother stood up and pulled me to unsteady feet.

"Take a walk with me, David. Let's find Li-Dan."

We walked along a winding path, passing dragons in various forms. All nodded their respect to the Dragon Mother and snickered at me as I stumbled along, leaning awkwardly against her. The path led up the plateau into a forest overgrown in a multitude of greens and daubed in light under the dense canopy. I heard the rush of water before we reached a stream spilling down a massive, flat slab of stone and then dropping into a basin.

A loud, clanging "wheeeee!" caused the Dragon Mother and me to look upstream in time to see a red dragon, scowling face and eyes blazing, catapult over a small waterfall, landing on his belly and sliding down the stream-covered slab to plop into the basin below. Splashing in the pool of water, the red dragon rang out a tinkling sound of laughter. Li-Dan, the Old Master, was playing ... again.

The Dragon Mother and I were still laughing when Li-Dan strutted up to us. He looked at me and yelled, "What's the matter, David? Have you never heard a dragon tintinnabulate before?"

"No, I haven't, and I see you are still playing your word game. It is good to see you, Li-Dan."

The air around Li-Dan shifted and shimmered for a few moments until Li-Dan the dragon was changed into Li-Dan the sage. Li-Dan offered his respects to the Dragon Mother before walking over and giving me a hearty, welcoming slap on the back. Li-Dan was in his traditional clothing, his portly body wrapped in a cream-colored robe trimmed in red silk. He looked every bit the wise "Old Master" this time.

Smiling broadly, Li-Dan said, "Please don't think me a cockalorum, but I am a dedicated player of life, for I am free and happy. And I am delighted you are here, in the In-Between."

The Dragon Mother guided us up a path that ran along the stream. The path cut through the verdant underbrush with exposed tree roots providing steps as we climbed to the waterfall. The water tumbled over a jutting boulder that formed the roof of a small cave. The path circled behind the falling water to the cave and continued into the forest beyond. The cave was shallow and hidden by the waterfall. A flat-topped stone nestled in front of the cave, and a similar stone lay beneath the falling water.

Li-Dan noticed me studying the cave and the stones. "I am a troglodyte, David; this is my cave, and these are my benches for meditation. I especially enjoy the bench under the beating water. It is exhilarating and energizing. The pounding of the water forces my internal focus on purification."

I reached my hand into the water and yanked it out in surprise.

"And the water is very cold," Li-Dan added.

"Li-Dan, I don't know how you can bear sitting in frigid water ... oh, wait! Yeah, you're a dragon." I was always good at stating the obvious.

"To be honest, David, the cold does give me the collywobbles sometimes," Li-Dan joked. It was just an excuse to use another funny-sounding word.

The Dragon Mother sat down on the stone bench in front of the cave and gestured for me to join her. Li-Dan, braving the collywobbles, flopped down on the bench under the freezing mountain shower. He immediately stilled into a meditational pose.

Looking tenderly upon Li-Dan, the Dragon Mother said softly, "Li-Dan is really not a flibbertigibbet, you know." Her golden eyes twinkled as she said it.

"I suppose not," I responded, having no idea what a flibbertigibbet was. Perhaps everyone in the In-Between plays the word game, I thought.

"Let me tell you a final story," she continued. The word "final" caused unease to grip me, but I kept quiet and listened carefully to what I assumed was the Dragon Mother's last lesson for me.

"Once there was a scholar of humble origins who worked as the Keeper of Archives for the Royal Court. Because of his position, he was able to study the ancient writings of the Yellow Emperor. The Yellow Emperor, if you recall, David, was instructed by the Golden Dragon."

And that would be you, I thought, remembering Li-Dan's words.

"Thus, this scholar learned of the wisdom from the Ages and became a renowned sage. He wrote extensively, sharing his insights into the nature of the world and people. Although he never opened a formal school, he attracted many students and devoted followers.

"His fame and skill as a sage came to the attention of the emperor, who sequestered him within his court. After a time, the sage grew weary of the court's moral decay and succeeded in a clever plan of escape to regain his independence. He ventured into the northern frontier mountains and lived as a hermit for several years in one of the numerous caverns, meditating and honing his understanding of the universe, which he eventually recorded as 'The Way of Caverns.' After a time, his followers found him and began living in the caverns, too. As his teachings took root, the faithful began to worship him as a god, calling him the 'Jade Emperor.' Disgusted by this and their inability to understand his teachings, he stole away one night and journeyed far as an itinerant, using various guises to avert detection.

"This worked for a time, for the sage lived with simplicity and humility, not drawing attention to himself. However, because his life moved in perfect harmony with the rest of creation, it was impossible to conceal his true nature. Envoys dispersed by the emperor found him and returned him to the court. Aware that the growing number of the sage's followers considered him the

Jade Emperor, the ruler of heaven, the emperor schemed to use control over the sage and his teaching to expand his rule.

"The sage was brought before the emperor, court ministers, and holy priests in a grand council to discuss this plan. With a copy of 'The Way of Caverns' in hand, they sought to attain consensus on a doctrine and canon of orthodoxy that would fulfill the emperor's desire for more power and control. A 'Creed of Caverns' was adopted to summarize the dogma of the new faith for the devout followers. The holy priests formulated an attractive set of sacred rites and rituals that would bind the lives of the populace to the new religion. The emperor was quite pleased and proclaimed 'The Way of Caverns' as the official and only acceptable religion of the land.

"Throughout the whole procedure, the sage stood quietly at the back of the council room, guarded on either side. When the proceedings were finalized, the emperor turned around and in an unctuous voice sneered, 'What say you, Jade Emperor?' "

"The sage stared into the emperor's eyes for a potent moment; then to the audible disbelief of the assembly, he turned his back on the emperor. The emperor, already discomfited by the sage's look, was shocked into silence at the insulting gesture. Before the guards could react, the sage slapped his hands together with a force that echoed through the hall, and to everyone's astonishment, a cave opening appeared on the wall, into which the sage stepped, never to be seen again.

"Naturally, the supernatural disappearance of the 'Jade Emperor' played well into the dogma of the new religion, but the emperor was profoundly affected by the sage's actions. Although his ministers and priests carried the plan forward, the emperor no longer had the heart for it and spent most of his time in quiet solitude in the Royal Garden until his death."

The Dragon Mother turned her gaze away from the waterfall to me. "Well?" she queried.

I looked at Li-Dan in the waterfall and stated the obvious again. "The sage was Li-Dan."

Li-Dan climbed out of the water and stood, dripping, in front of the Dragon Mother and me. His robe inexplicably wicked dry as he said, "That was pauciloquent of you, David, but you understood the story, yes?"

It appeared to be a rhetorical question, so I nodded and said nothing. The Dragon Mother took hold of my hand. I sighed. Li-Dan put his arm around my shoulder. "David," he said, "I have enjoyed being your goombah, but now it is time for you to go into the cave and walk widdershins nine times."

The Dragon Mother, seeing my confusion, said quietly. "Walk in a counterclockwise circle nine times, David."

The unease I felt became sadness, as the sting of tears blurred my vision. I looked deeply into the Dragon Mother's eyes, tears beseeching solace. Seeing my distress, her golden eyes blazed for a moment, and a wave of serenity swept over me.

Softly, she said, "Painting will allow you to reach out to the truths in the world. By expressing the vitality of life in your paintings, you will find harmony within yourself, and you will acquire a passion for the sublime beauty in the workings of nature. Allow your art to be a spiritual experience that enriches you and those around you. Do this, and love will grow within you until it manifests in your every thought and action."

"Yes, thank you, Dragon Mother." I understood her instructions. The stories and lessons from the Dragon Mother and Li-Dan over the months had not been in vain. Whether I could realize these virtuous ideals, I did not know. At least now I had a direction and an intention to guide my painting and my life.

The Dragon Mother teased a look at me. "David, what color are you? You are a painter. You should know what color interacts with your rhythms and is ingrained in your essence. So, what color are you?"

Being a painter, I delight in all colors, but I have always known the color that resonates strongly in me, that gives me the greatest joy when I use it. "Blue, Dragon Mother. I am blue."

"Of course you are," she beamed. "Blue as the color of the azure dragon, who roars out of the east, driven by the might of the northeast wind, and who rises out of the churning ocean, to bring the nourishing rains of spring upon the land."

Another aphorism, but I really liked that one. The Dragon Mother, holding my hand, and Li-Dan, arm still around my shoulder, walked me to the cave opening. Entering the cave's dimness alone, I looked back at the Dragon Mother when she began to glow golden and whispered in the dark to me, "Never forget our connection."

How could I forget, I thought, as I walked in counterclockwise circles on the cave's red clay floor. It was as if I was turning a cosmic clock back in time as I circled round and round. The cave began to vibrate and blaze blue in increasing intensity, until finishing the ninth circle, I collapsed into darkness.

From faraway, a bonging sound zoomed into my head, awakening me to consciousness. Disoriented, I peered into the gloom. I was in a room and sitting on a bed, my back propped on pillows against the wall. There were large, open windows at either end of the bed. A breeze smelling of salted air blew the gossamer curtains. I was back in my bedroom and sitting in meditational pose exactly as I was months ago when the Dragon Mother first drew me into the In-Between.

Sitting very still, I replayed the stories and events of the last few months in my mind. Was I awakening from a vivid dream or from a vision? There was an insubstantial quality to the recollections, like a surreal fantasy. Baffled, I gazed out the window at the full moon, its ghostly light illuminating the night sky and shadowing palm trees swaying in the breeze, and a thought flashed into my mind: "Never forget our connection."

Shifting back from the In-Between to the world must have addled my mind. Resuming meditational pose, I repeated, "Never forget our connection" as a mantra, until a golden light flashed in my inner eye, and all the events and truths revealed to me by the Dragon Mother and Li-Dan roared through my consciousness like a dragon in a storm — and then there was an image!

Running down to the studio, I put a canvas on the easel and rapidly executed a painting called "The Artist as an Azure Dragon Rising." As I was applying the finishing touches, a familiar voice inserted itself into my internal conversation once more. Words with a delicate undertone, like coins jingling together, formed in my mind.

"When you create a painting that you can walk into, do so, and I will be waiting for you."

Filled with happiness, I laughed. "As you say, Dragon Mother."

Azure Dragon Rising

Glossary
Li-Dan's Fun Words

Bamboozle — To hoodwink, trick, or make a fool of.

Bloviate — To speak pompously or brag.

Bumfuzzle — To confuse, perplex, or fluster.

Cockalorum — A small, haughty man, menial, yet self-important.

Cockamamie — Absurd, outlandish, foolish, or unbelievable.

Codswallop — Nonsense, balderdash, rubbish.

Collywobbles — Butterflies in the stomach, or a bellyache.

Discombobulate — To confuse, befuddle, or perplex.

Flabbergast — To overwhelm with bewilderment.

Flibbertigibbet — An offbeat, skittish, or scatterbrained person.

Gaberlunzie — A wandering beggar.

Gardyloo — A warning shout for something falling from above.

Gobbledygook — Nonsense, meaningless, balderdash.

Gobsmack — To astonish or surprise.

Gongoozle — To observe things idly, or stare at.

Goombah — An older protector or advisor.

Jargogle — To confuse or jumble up.

Mumpsimus — Person obstinately adhering to obviously wrong old ways.

Pauciloquent — Using few words when speaking.

Snollygoster — A shrewd person who cannot be trusted.

Splendiferous — Beautiful, splendid.

Tarradiddle — A trivial fib or pretentious nonsense.

Tintinnabulate — To ring, tinkle, toll, or sound like bells.
Troglodyte — Someone who lives in a cave.
Widdershins — In a contrary or counterclockwise direction.

The Dragon Mother

Here Comes the Sun

About the Author/Artist
David Hansford

David Hansford has a degree in chemistry from Oglethorpe University in Atlanta. David began his art studies at the Instituto Allende in San Miguel de Allende, Mexico, and finished at Georgia State University in Atlanta under the tutelage of his art sensei, James Sitton.

David has studied Okinawan karate for many years and authored two books on the science behind traditional martial arts — *P.A.T.H. Approach to Effective Self Defense* and *Part 2, Kiko*. His spiritual animal, assigned by his sensei based on the interactions of his body, mind, and spirit in training, is the dragon.

David's philosophy of life and painting is informed by these influences. He believes the sacredness and revelations about the universe can be found in the small and insignificant in nature. David advocates for a contemporary art world where artists in all media return to the primordial purpose of art, which is to make the magic that connects the seen with the unseen, to fathom the dual nature of reality and to understand the shifting balance of the physical world with forces that affect it. From this exploration comes an understanding of the harmony in the universe, and out of this beauty flows.

David lives on a barrier island in northeast Florida with his wife, Laura. His two sons, Wolff and Adam, born and raised with salt in their hair, still make the beach their home. David hopes always to walk the surf.